From Two Islands

Stories from Ireland and Australia

From Two Islands

Stories from Ireland and Australia

selected by
Emer Ryan and Clive Newman

FREMANTLE ARTS CENTRE PRESS

First published in Australia 2000 by
FREMANTLE ARTS CENTRE PRESS
PO Box 158, North Fremantle
Western Australia 6159.
http://www.facp.iinet.net.au

and WOLFHOUND PRESS
68 Mountjoy Square
Dublin 1
Ireland

Copyright © individual contributors.

This book is copyright. Apart from any fair dealing for the purpose of
private study, research, criticism or review, as permitted under the
Copyright Act, no part may be reproduced by any process without written
permission. Enquiries should be made to the publisher.

Fremantle Arts Centre Press Edition Cover Designer Marion Duke.
Production Coordinator Cate Sutherland.
Typeset by Fremantle Arts Centre Press.
Printed by PK Print, Hamilton Hill, Western Australia.

National Library of Australia
Cataloguing in Publication Data

> From two islands: stories for young readers from Ireland and Australia.
>
> ISBN 1 86368 282 1.
>
> 1. Short stories, Irish. 2. Short stories, Australian. 3. Young adult fiction.
> I Ryan, Emer. II. Newman, Clive Douglas.
>
> 823.0108

British Library
Cataloguing in Publication Data

> A catalogue record for this book is avaiable from the British Library.
>
> ISBN 0-86327-787-X

The State of Western Australia has made an investment in this project
through ArtsWA in association with the Lotteries Commission.

Wolfhound Press receives financial assistance from the Arts Council/An
Chomhairle Ealaion, Dublin.

Contents

FROM THE SMALL ISLAND

Margot Bosonnet	The Great Abominable Snowgull	9
Jim Halligan and John Newman	Bin There, Done That	26
Aislinn O'Loughlin	El Kid	41
Larry O'Loughlin	The Survivor	60
Mark O'Sullivan	The Wishbone	76
Cora Harrison	Millennia	91

FROM THE BIG ISLAND

David Caddy	Sabotage	105
Deborah Lisson	Popocatapetl	116
Jenny Coote	BIG Weekend	127
Warren Flynn	An Angel at Cow Town	135
Kim Scott	Dallas' Dad	149
Elaine Forrestal	Bitten by the Millennium Bug	157

Biographical Notes 169

FROM THE SMALL ISLAND

The Great Abominable Snowgull

MARGOT BOSONNET

DAY 1

We thought it was the end of the world, the Apocalypse. Well, who could blame us, after the chaos of the preceding week?

For six days Arctic storms had swept the country, though it was only early October. Most of Donegal was without electricity. Half the roads in the country were blocked by fallen trees. Living in the midlands, the bowl of Ireland, we'd got off lightly. Oh, we'd had bitter gales and some early snow, but our lights were still on and our telephones working.

The last storm was forecast to blow itself out around midnight; so when we woke to silence, instead of the howling of the wind down our old chimney, we thought the worst was over. Little did we know it was just about to begin.

Mam bustled about getting breakfast double-quick. People were always in a hurry in our house. She opened the curtains, but, seeing it was black outside, said, 'Goodness, the dark mornings are drawing in already!' before shutting them again.

Dad was gobbling down his toast, edgy and anxious. He'd been edgy and anxious for weeks. His computers kept crashing at work and the area manager was breathing down his neck. Everything had been fine until the computers were made Y2K-compliant. Since then they'd been playing up.

He glanced at his watch and shot out of the chair — 'Dear God! Is that the time?' In a single movement he slid into his coat, grabbed his briefcase and slammed the door behind him as he left.

Before Mam or I could even draw a breath, there came the most terrifying sounds — muffled thuddings and scratchings — and the roof creaked alarmingly. Then Dad was banging on the door and screaming, 'Let me in! Let me in! Oh, quick!'

I ran to the door. Dad catapulted in as soon as I opened it a bit. I slammed it shut again, with all the strength of my back against it. I hadn't even dared to look out.

Dad lay huddled on the floor where he had fallen, still clutching his briefcase, looking ... well ... *crumpled*.

'It's the end of the world,' he sobbed. 'The end of the world.'

'It can't be,' said Mam wildly. 'It's only October ... the millennium's not till January!'

I'd often wondered how I would feel at the end of the world. Now I know. Calm. Calm as anything. Totally accepting — like I was in the middle of one of those weird, surrealistic dreams where the oddest things seem normal.

Dad was making no effort to get up off the floor.

'What's out there?' Mam had panic all over her face.

'Horrible stuff! The world is gone — it's all filled up with ... with ... *stuff*.'

'We're snowbound?'

'It's not snow — oh, definitely not snow!'

'You mean we're buried in something else?' I asked.

Dad nodded.

'Fallout, like Pompeii — the way it was buried in cinders?'

He nodded again and closed his eyes, his lips trembling.

So we were doomed. There didn't seem to be anything else to say. I helped Dad up and into an armchair. He sat there, staring blankly into space.

The baby started to cry, jolting us back to some normality. Annie was only three months old. Mam fetched her from the bedroom, then sat down on the sofa, jumper up, and started to feed her.

I went back to finishing my breakfast. Well, what else was there to do?

For a long time the silence was broken only by the baby's slurping.

Then — *Rrring! rrring!*

The sound of the telephone made us jump. It was Auntie Madge. She lives two fields away from us.

'Jessie ... Jessie ... are you okay?'

'I'm okay,' I said.

'Is your mother okay? Is Annie okay?'

'They're fine.'

'Thank God!'

Nothing about my Dad. Oh, well ...

'Are you okay too?' I asked. (That sort of conversation is catching.)

'Of course I am. Why wouldn't I be? Put your mother on.'

I pulled the phone over to the sofa, switching on the speaker as I did so. Auntie Madge's voice boomed out all over the room.

'Dee! You're all right, so?'

'We're fine. What's going on, Madge?'

'Well ...' Auntie Madge seemed lost for words at first. 'I hate to tell you, Dee, but there's a big bird sitting on your roof.'

'A big *bird*?'

'Really big. As a matter of fact, I can't see your house at all. It's completely covered.'

Mam didn't reply to this. She eyed my dad, then me. The implication was clear: it was the end of the world, and Auntie Madge had flipped. So, humouring her sister, Mam asked carefully, 'What kind of a bird?'

'It's white ... with a huge, curving beak. It

looks like a giant seagull.'

A giant seagull. Now we knew.

'Look, I'll get on to the police right away,' Auntie Madge said. 'You just sit tight; that thing looks dangerous. The police will know what to do.' She slammed the phone down.

Annie had fallen asleep. We sat there waiting for the whole absurd situation to somehow go back to normal.

The next call only confirmed the bizarreness. It was from our local Garda Superintendent.

We seemed to have a bit of a problem, he explained. A big bird. He was seeking advice and would be in touch again.

The next call was for Dad.

'Where the hell are you, Humphries?' The area manager's voice was irate. My dad explained.

The manager freaked. 'My business is going down the tubes,' he screamed, 'and you're worried about a *bird* on your roof? Get in here at once or you're fired!'

Dad put the phone down quite calmly. Then he started to laugh. He laughed until the tears ran down his face.

Mam wasn't laughing at all. 'I never did like that man,' she said.

So, basically, that was it. We were stuck, until somebody came up with an idea or else the big bird flew away again.

I went up to my bedroom to think.

I should explain that we live in an old thatched cottage on the edge of town. It used to belong to Dad's great-aunt. She did a bit of market gardening in the surrounding fields. Dad used to help her with it when he was a boy, so she left him the lot in her will, hoping he'd continue the business. But he went into insurance instead. Now the far field was let for grazing, and the field around our house was mostly a wilderness, with overgrown greenhouses. We just kept a bit of lawn, back and front, that could be mown easily.

The cottage has only one large main room, which serves as kitchen, dining room and lounge. It's nice, all the same, with the roof-beams showing and a huge fireplace. We don't use the fireplace much, as we have central heating — Mam was always too busy with committees to be raking out ashes. The main bedroom is at one end of the house, and I have the loft room over it — right under the roof, with a small window in the gable end.

I sat on my bed and considered the situation. It was quiet here. The only sound was a soft *thud-thud* somewhere in the distance. At least I was getting time off school. I'd just gone into secondary, and it was a pain — not the school itself, but all this sudden talk about futures, careers, exams, study. After Christmas we'd have to decide on our subjects for the Junior Cert. The teachers were going on with all this rubbish about the coming millennium being a whole new era of opportunity, the world being our oyster and all that. But how were we supposed to pick subjects when we didn't even know what we wanted to do with our lives?

Anyway, I thought the world was in a pretty rotten state, myself. New technology and instant worldwide communication hadn't stopped the wars or the famines, or solved the problems of time bombs like Chernobyl and Sellafield. What made anyone think there *was* a future out there for us?

One thing I did know for certain: I was never going into insurance.

Downstairs had become a madhouse. The whole town was trying to ring us up. There was no sign of lunch being made, so I opened a tin of beans and put a bowlful each in front of Mam and Dad. They ate up every scrap.

The Garda Superintendent phoned back to say that, since we were all in good health, he was going to defer any decisions until the morning. Hopefully the big bird would fly away before then, and the problem would be solved. If it didn't, he was going to call out the fire brigade and have them hose the bird off our roof.

Mam cheered up a lot after that. It was only one day, after all, and the poor people of Donegal had been without electricity for nearly a week, which was worse, a lot worse. We even had the telly — luckily our TV aerial is attached to a shed in the field, or the big bird would have banjaxed it.

Dad was in a strange mood, though. The area manager had phoned back, in a state of high excitement. What a fortunate occurrence for an insurance company! Think of all the publicity! My dad could have as much time off as he needed. They'd taken photographs of the bird already, to use in the firm's advertisements. Dad could do interviews for them later.

Dad went very quiet after that. 'They think they own me!' he said to Mam. Then he started rummaging through his great-aunt's collection of gardening encyclopaedias, as if he was looking for answers.

Late in the afternoon, we heard the faint sound of a helicopter overhead. I was busy getting the dinner, since nobody else had offered. I made a huge six-egg omelette, with fried frozen chips and onions stirred in. We all had some and it was scrumptious.

I went to bed early. There was nothing on telly and I was fed up with computer games. I thought that if I could go to sleep, morning would somehow come quicker.

Then it was eleven o'clock at night and Mam was shaking me awake, telling me to come downstairs. We were on Sky TV! Some enterprising photographer had hired a helicopter to get a bird's-eye view of the bird, and had sold the film to Sky News. There was our house — or, rather, there was a gigantic white bird sitting in a field of snow where our house should have been. The camouflage was superb.

'Look, it's got its wings down over the sides of the house,' Mam said to Dad 'That's what you ran into outside the door!'

I sat staring at the big bird, mesmerised. Somehow, in my heart of hearts, I hadn't quite believed in it until then. The sheer size, the beauty of the thing, left me speechless.

They showed the same film clips three times in the next hour, so we knew there wouldn't be anything more until the morning.

I could hardly sleep after that, thinking about the big bird — just an arm's length away, on the other side of the thatch. We were folded in under its wings like a clutch of fledglings in a nest.

Thud … thud … thud … That sound again!

Suddenly I realised what it was. The TV pictures — the bird facing north … My gable window faced north; so I was right beneath the breast of the big bird, listening to its heartbeat. *Thud … thud … thud …*

I drifted off again into an uneasy sleep.

DAY 2

That morning all hell broke loose.

Sky News was here, with its camera crews, at the crack of dawn. So were the eco-warriors, with a man claiming to be a Greenpeace watchdog, and a horde of sightseers. The eco-warriors had been looking for a new cause to support ever since their defeat in the Glen of the Downs, where they'd tried to prevent a road through an ecologically sensitive area being turned into a six-lane highway. The police had their work cut out trying to contain them all.

We were up at the crack of dawn too, clustered around the telly. It was the only way we could find out what was happening to our own house.

At nine o'clock, Deadly Earnest arrived.

His real name is Dr Dudley Ernest, but everyone calls him Deadly Earnest (as in deadly, brilliant, cool). He's a world-famous ornithologist, specialising in Arctic birds. He's seventy-two years old and he looks scatty, with wild wisps of white hair falling to his shoulders and a permanent laugh on his face. Scatty? He's anything but! A retired professor, he still lectures at universities all over the world.

Anyway, he was wildly excited.

'Fifty years!' he kept saying. 'Fifty years since the last sighting. I'd given up hope — I thought it was extinct!'

'You recognise it, then?' the Sky News interviewer asked.

'Of course! Of course! It's the Great Abominable Snowgull. I've spent most of my life looking for this bird. What a beauty! What magnificence ... but what a *tragedy* to find it here!'

He went on to explain that the bird belonged in the high Arctic regions around the North Pole. It was named after the Abominable Snowman, because nobody could prove that existed either, in spite of reported sightings. The Snowgull was said to build its nest on ice floes, using ropes from the riggings of old sailing ships.

'Not too many sailing ships around these days.' The Sky TV interviewer was sceptical.

'No. That's why it's almost extinct,' said Deadly Earnest sadly.

Asked why the bird should have landed on

our house, the Professor thought that was entirely logical. Blown off course and disorientated by the storms, the bird had settled on our thatched roof because it looked like its own nest — especially with the whitewashed walls of the cottage underneath, and the snow on the ground.

At this point the interview was interrupted by the arrival of a fire engine, sirens blaring. Our Garda Superintendent explained that the fire brigade was going to hose the bird off the roof.

Deadly Earnest's euphoria vanished. As a matter of fact, he got quite shirty.

'That bird is a rare endangered species!' he spluttered.

'That cottage is a listed building,' countered the Superintendent. 'Last thatched roof in this county, as a matter of fact. And there's a baby to be considered — four people who are my responsibility.'

'Interfere with that bird and you'll be responsible to the whole world,' warned Deadly Earnest, waving an arm towards the Sky TV cameras.

The eco-warriors got in on the act, chanting 'Save our bird! Save our bird!' The Superintendent was left with little choice. He told the fire brigade to back off and wait down the road.

'And the rest of them too!' insisted Deadly Earnest. 'I don't know what you think you're doing, permitting a crowd like that to gather so close to such a rare specimen …'

The man from Greenpeace quietly interrupted to enquire if food supplies had been arranged for the bird.

Things were getting nasty. But the Superintendent wasn't a superintendent for nothing. The situation clearly required a change of tactics.

The crowd was shifted a quarter of a mile down the road and firmly corralled behind barriers — Deadly Earnest, eco-warriors, Mr Greenpeace, and the Sky TV people included. Soon after that, the Superintendent announced that a certain helicopter company had offered to airlift in crates of fresh fish, free of charge, to feed the bird. It seems that you can be prosecuted for flying over an endangered species without a permit.

We, of course, were still stuck inside, but the regular Sky News broadcasts kept us up to date. Just as well, because Auntie Madge was too busy to talk to us any more. The crowds were now parked on her doorstep, and she was charging fifty pence a cup for tea.

Dad was finding things difficult. On Day 1, his mood had swung from sheer terror to confusion to hysterical laughter, then to anger, then back to confusion again. On the morning of Day 2, he made one brief attempt to regain control.

Deadly Earnest had just been explaining about the big bird and its Arctic wilderness.

'Stuff and nonsense!' Dad roared at the TV. 'There's no such thing as a wilderness any more. You couldn't *fart* at the North Pole without the armies of half a dozen countries knowing. How could a thing like that *disappear* for fifty years?'

I stared at Mam until it became clear that she wasn't going to comment on Dad's use of what she usually called 'coarse language'.

'Well, where did it come from, then?' I demanded.

There was a long pause. Then Dad sort of collapsed, visibly shrinking into the depths of the armchair, his bravado suddenly swept away by the enormity of the question.

'I don't know,' he said.

He didn't know. I didn't know. Mam didn't know. The armies of half a dozen countries obviously didn't know. Nobody knew ... at least, nobody on Earth. I got out my school atlas and brooded over the Arctic Circle.

An airlift of fresh mackerel arrived at half past three. There were plenty of arguments about how it could be fed to the bird safely — in other words, without the bearers being considered food as well. The eco-warriors offered to carry the crates in relays; they were used to sacrificing themselves. Deadly Earnest wasn't sure if the bird would even eat, in its exhausted state.

He needn't have worried. As soon as the crate-carriers came within range, the bird's beak swooped down, and it was already gobbling up the mackerel as the eco-warriors dropped the crate and fled. It ate the lot, crate after crate of the stuff. Its appetite was phenomenal. Finally, when all the mackerel was gone, buckets of water were brought to it too.

Deadly Earnest was dead excited. The bird was obviously in good shape, in spite of everything.

'Tomorrow we'll tag it,' he declared. 'We'll fit an electronic bleeper, so that we can monitor it wherever it goes — find out where it lives. Perhaps there's even a mate ...'

'How will you do that?' the Sky News reporter asked.

'We'll use a tranquilliser dart to knock it out, then fit the bleeper quickly while it's unconscious. I've been in touch with an expert in the field. He'll be here first thing in the morning.'

Now, I knew it was the correct scientific thing to do; but that was when I started to feel sorry for the big bird. It hadn't harmed us at all. Mam seemed quite happy to relax at home with Annie instead of rushing out to committees; Dad was absorbed in the gardening encyclopaedias again; and I was okay. But the Great Abominable Snowgull ... would it be okay too, after all this — after tomorrow? Suppose it never woke up again after it was tagged. Suppose it died!

That night I was lulled to sleep once more by the soft thud-thudding of its heartbeat, and I had the most beautiful dream. We were high above the Arctic Circle, me and the big bird, gliding over mountains of ice and wild wastelands lit by brilliant, flickering rainbow lights. We were rising and falling carelessly in the cold currents of air. Rising and falling, rising and falling ...

Rising from the depths of the dream, I was suddenly awake and listening to those steady heartbeats — *thud ... thud ... thud ...* Suddenly I knew that I couldn't leave things like this. I had to try to warn the bird.

Slipping out of bed, I crossed over to the window and, opening it a little, carefully slid my arm outside. It felt like I'd put my hand into a feather pillow, only softer. Soft and warm. Gently I stroked the downy feathers with my fingers, and I felt a stirring overhead.

'Big bird,' I whispered urgently, 'go! Go tonight! Or tomorrow you'll belong to them. Go! Go!' With all the strength of my mind I willed the bird to understand my message, to understand the danger it was in. *Go! Go! Go!*

I don't know how long I stood there, energy draining out of me with each urging effort, but finally I couldn't keep it up any longer. Exhausted, I closed the window and went back to bed, falling at once into a deep, dreamless sleep.

DAY 3

The first dim light of morning was framed in the square of my bedroom window. Overhead the roof creaked, and dust trickled down onto my face. The bird was on the move!

I was out of bed in an instant and racing down the stairs to the front door, desperate to be there in time.

Outside, I scanned the darkness of the fields. The bird was already far off in the western sky. Oblivious to the cold, I watched it circle to the south. In the strange half-light, for just a moment, ages suddenly slipped away; the moving shadow was some huge primeval creature, and this place as unfamiliar as a prehistoric landscape risen from the depths of time.

I thought I'd lost it then, that it would keep on going; but instead it circled back again, towards our house ... towards me ... gleaming whitely as it emerged from the edge of the night.

It sailed high overhead, filling the sky like a beautiful paper kite. Then, with long sinuous sweeps of its enormous wings, it drew away. Barefoot in the snow, I watched it fade into the distant skies.

Then it was gone, heading north for home.

EPILOGUE

It changed our lives, the big bird.

Dad said it was a sign. He gave up insurance and started to resurrect the garden. He's growing organic vegetables and herbs. They'll fetch big prices, he reckons, in these days of genetically modified crops and irradiated food. He's much happier, too.

So is Mam. She's stopped rushing around and is helping Dad with the greenhouses. She's been investigating courses in horticulture for when Annie's a bit older.

As for me, Deadly Earnest is a pal of mine now, and I've found my direction in life. I've been looking up the subjects — glaciology, climatology, glacial geomorphology. For the big bird left me feeling like I'd been called, somehow, and I know that someday I'll follow it to its

Arctic home — to the tundra, the deserts, the wilderness of pack ice — and help to make its environment secure.

And maybe Dad's right, and it was a sign; for as long as something so strange, so beautiful, so utterly *unexplainable* still exists in the world, then there's hope for us all.

Bin There, Done That

JIM HALLIGAN AND JOHN NEWMAN

My ears were still ringing from the deafening sound of the crash. The thing that had landed, whatever it was, had cut a furrow through the low-tide mud, just missing a large rock covered in seaweed. I slithered and slipped my way across the oozy, slimy mud to see what had caused the commotion. For once, there wasn't a bird to be seen or heard along the shore.

That was when I saw the spaceship.

Mind you, it didn't look much like anything I'd ever seen on TV. It was a small dull-grey cylinder, for all the world like a battered old dustbin. Steam rose from the wet mud around it.

I nearly dropped my binoculars and bird book when the lid popped open. Yes, it was just like a dustbin lid, except that it was on hinges and tiny lights flashed on the inside of it. A small purplish-green hand fumbled its way out of the opening, and a small purplish-green alien followed it.

I couldn't move — but then, my feet were stuck in the mud. Anyway, he — or she — didn't look scary. He or she (I never found out which) was about half my height, pear-shaped, with two small purple eyes on stalks sticking out of the top of its (I suppose) head. At least it had a human number of arms and legs.

'Nice to see you, to see you nice! Yes sir, it really, truly is!' it chirped at me. 'It's really lovely to see you here today — and, boy, do I have questions for you!'

'Right,' I gasped. I was beginning to wonder where it had learned to speak English.

'Here's a nice little starter for you. Could you tell me … your name?'

'Alan,' I mumbled, trying to unstick my feet. 'Is that your spaceship?'

'*Was*, Al, *was*. Slight problem with fuel. Should have stuck with my old brand,' it told me. 'So here's the six-million-dollar question … Can you help me make another?'

We trudged off in the direction of town. I couldn't think of anywhere to go but home, and, I have to admit it, I felt pretty shaken. My plans for the day hadn't included acting as a breakdown service for stranded aliens. I mean, what was I supposed to do? I was just a kid. What did I know about building spaceships?

I glanced over at my new companion, trotting along beside me on its short legs. My head was bursting with questions, and I began to ask them.

It turned out that the alien's name was Asb, and it had a breathtaking knowledge of washing powders, fabric conditioners and heaven knows what else. Asb could also hum the theme tune from every quiz show I'd ever heard of, and plenty that I hadn't.

As we approached the edge of town, I began to worry about how I was going to explain just who Asb was. Would it be safe to introduce people to an alien? Would someone hurt it?

I was mulling these thoughts over in my head when my new friend stopped in its tracks. Its eyes were out on stalks — well, they were anyway, but I could tell that Asb had spotted something fascinating.

There, by a gateway, with only a few flies buzzing over it, stood a new dustbin. It was one of those ones with wheels on the end. It gleamed invitingly.

'Wow ...' Asb gasped slowly. 'A deluxe model!'

Asb looked like someone taking a first serious look at a Ferrari. I glanced about nervously as it inspected every detail, such as there were.

'Um, Asb ...' I tried to sound coaxing.

Just then, I heard footsteps crunching on the gravel on the other side of the gate. I grabbed my alien friend and took off as fast as our legs would allow.

'Not ... a good idea ... to be seen,' I panted, as we turned in to the quiet side road which led to my house.

'Okey-dokey-cokey!' agreed Asb, trotting

along beside me. The little guy (or girl) seemed quite happy to jog along and tell me a bit more about himself — herself, itself, whatever.

It seems that space is full of creatures like Asb. They call themselves 'Planet-Hoppers', and they like hanging about near Earth so that they can pick up all the satellite TV channels — that explained Asb's grasp of English. The other reason why Earth is a good spot is because we humans tend to leave lots of junk from our rocket launches in space, and it comes in dead handy for making repairs, or even for building whole new spacecraft. Occasionally, Planet-Hoppers actually land on Earth to see what they can find. Asb talked about scrapyards as though they were some kind of wonderland. It seems the spaceship which had just crashed was originally found in a dump near Paris.

I was flummoxed.

'But — but you need all kinds of … stuff … to make a spaceship!' I protested.

'Nah!' Asb told me. 'A few bits of wire and a nice comfy box, and Bob's your uncle.' Its eyes twinkled. 'Stick a few flashing lights here and there, and it goes faster. Piece of cake!'

There was no one at home when we walked into the back garden. Asb paused to inspect the orderly rows of vegetables which were my father's pride and joy. It ran a finger tentatively along the gleaming side of Dad's greenhouse.

'Dad's big into gardening,' I explained.

'Takes all sorts, Al,' was Asb's only comment.

My mind was working overtime as I led the

purple-green stranger into the house. What were we going to use to make a new spaceship? How were we going to get what we needed? And how was I going to get all this done without my parents finding out?

'I've got thirty-eight pounds and ninety-five pence in my money-box,' I called over my shoulder, as I put down my binoculars and book. 'That should get us ... Asb?'

There was no sign of Asb. It had wandered off.

'Asb?' I called. No answer.

Then I heard a whoop of joy coming from the garage. I ran out to see what had got Asb so excited.

I found it standing triumphantly on top of an old washing machine that Mum had dumped there ages ago. A box full of Christmas decorations had been flung open, and a string of fairy lights was uncoiled across the garage floor.

'That'll do nicely!' declared Asb, brandishing Dad's socket wrench.

Right. Dustbins, washing machines — it didn't seem to matter to Asb. I assumed the little alien *could* build a spaceship, seeing as it was able to fly one ... or, at least, crash one. I scratched my head and got to work as an assistant mechanic.

I can't say I understood what we were doing, but it was great fun. Asb expertly gutted the washing machine and fiddled about confidently with old bits of coloured wire. The comments it made as it worked left me feeling a bit doubtful, though.

'Black wire? I hate black wire! Out it goes!'

'Stick a few lights there … Lovely!'

'Stop the lights! We've hit the jackpot! Washing powder! Great fuel — and, hey, it's biological. Super!'

'Ooh, a twiddly knob! Just give it a twist … Great!'

We found an old pair of Mum's tights that had got lost in the machine at some point.

'Hey! A seat belt! Clunk, click, every trip!' Asb was delighted. Still, Mum wouldn't miss them …

Time was flying. I completely lost track of it. My head snapped up as I heard the sound of the car coming up the driveway. My parents were back.

'Quick!' I hissed. 'My mum and dad are here! Are you nearly done?'

'No problemo,' Asb said confidently. 'We're ready for a test drive.'

'What! Now?'

'No time like the present, Al. No time like the present. Here goes …'

With that — and I'll always remember it — Asb pressed a button on the front of the washing machine — the one for 'boil wash', I believe. There was a whirring noise, then a grinding …

(The car doors slammed …)

Then a strange whine …

(I heard the sound of approaching footsteps …)

A few sparks …

(Keys jingled in the door …)

The washing machine shuddered violently. Sparks danced out of the top, followed by a few small bubbles. The bubbles burst, leaving wisps of foul-smelling smoke. The drum inside the machine started to spin with a horrible grinding noise. The washing machine's casing began to bulge in places. A screw shot out of the back and pinged off the garage ceiling.

'Asb?' I was feeling fairly panicky. 'What now?'

The little alien's stalk-eyes dipped slightly, as though it was frowning in deep concern.

'We take cover,' it announced, grabbing my arm. '*Now!*'

My father had just reached the kitchen window, and was gazing with pride at his beloved garden, when it happened.

The back door of the garage disintegrated into a million splinters, and the stainless-steel drum of the old washing machine shot out into the garden. Well, into my dad's vegetable patch, actually. It whizzed up a row of prize specimen cabbages and then skipped across to decimate the carrots. The leeks were next; then the lettuces, the potatoes, the beets, the celery ... Are you getting the picture here?

On its last circuit of the garden, the deranged washing-drum gave the rose bushes the pruning from hell — and then headed straight for the greenhouse.

One ordinary-sized washing-drum, one fairly large greenhouse. You'd think at least some of the panes of glass would have survived, wouldn't you?

The steel drum came to a final, mangled halt at ... no, around ... no, through the barbecue. The new barbecue.

Asb and I watched in horrified fascination through the shattered doorway.

My new friend muttered, 'Should have gone for the delicates wash cycle.' Nice one, Asb.

My father shuffled out to what had once been his garden.

There are a lot of words to describe what the garden looked like. Some of them are even polite. Maybe the best word to use would be 'coleslaw'. Every single vegetable had been shredded beyond anything that even an experienced cook could have identified.

Dad stooped to pick something up off the ground. It was a Christmas fairy light.

Then he saw me.

Asb ducked out of sight. I walked out to the garden.

'I can explain,' I assured Dad, my hands raised in a soothing gesture. 'I … I …' I tried to figure out what I was going to say next. What *could* I say? 'I … I …' My eyelids began to flicker. 'I can't explain.'

There wasn't much else I could say, really.

However, there was lots that Mum and Dad wanted to say.

'Maniac … irresponsible … criminally insane … your father's pride and joy … tomorrow's gardening festival … Dad's best chance of winning in years … hopes dashed …'

I felt sorry for Dad. I really did. I'd have felt even sorrier for him if he and Mum hadn't grounded me indefinitely and made it clear that my pocket money would be nonexistent until all of the damage was paid for. Glancing over my shoulder at the garden, I figured they'd probably be taking money out of my old-age pension.

Later that evening, mulling things over in my room, I heard a tapping at my window. It was Asb.

'Slight setback there,' it admitted, climbing in through the window. A master of understatement, our Asb.

We sat down to review our options. I was banned from going near the garage. My £38.95 was gone, and so were my chances of getting any more cash. I couldn't get Asb a wastepaper basket, let alone a decent-sized dustbin to make a new spaceship out of.

I could hear my father, outside, declaring that he had no intention of going anywhere near the gardening competition. His prize cabbages were in tatters, and so were his dreams of glory. I felt a fresh pang of guilt.

Asb must have noticed my despondent look.

'Now, now. Cheer up, cheer up. Don't despair, don't despair!' it cajoled cheerfully.

'Get lost, get lost!' I snapped back, my temper rising. 'I feel sorry for a stranded alien who goes flying around in a *dustbin*, for heaven's sake ... and what do I get? The garden's a disaster zone; my dad's suicidal; my mum is ready to strangle me; I'm in the doghouse *forever* — and the best you can come up with is "cheer up"? Bloomin'"cheer *up*"?'

Asb had the decency to look crestfallen. Its eye-stalks sort of wilted, and its arms hung limply by its sides. It slumped down on the floor. It looked for all the world like a giant, tragic, heartbroken avocado.

A giant, tragic, heartbroken ... avocado ...

A giant avocado ...

Somewhere, in the dimmest, darkest corner of my mind, a tiny light-bulb began to glimmer. An idea, an *outrageous* idea, was forming there.

Did I dare? Would Asb be able to pull it off?

*

The annual gardening festival was to be held in a small hall at the back of a church on the other side of town. Getting there was going to be a bit of a problem, but I did have the whole evening and the whole night in my room to plan things out.

'When the going gets tough, the tough go shopping,' was the sum total of the advice that Asb had to offer after hours of pondering. Great help. Mind you, it did remind me that I had an old shopping bag in the bottom of my wardrobe, for storing my football gear in. It'd do nicely to carry Asb in.

Leaving by the door was a total non-starter. Just about every floorboard in our house creaks like an army of lovesick frogs. I'd have been recaptured, re-lectured and re-grounded before you could say 'juvenile delinquent'. The window was the only way.

'A window of opportunity,' Asb assured me,

peering down from the ledge.

'Thanks,' I muttered through gritted teeth, as I stared down the two-storey drop at the garden below — or what was left of it. The dew on the grass glistened in the early-morning sun.

Asb suddenly leaped off the windowsill and dropped to the ground below. It bounced twice and rolled a little before coming to rest in the middle of the battle-scarred lawn.

'Come on down!' it whispered up cheerfully.

I sighed. Climbing gingerly out onto the window-ledge, I caught hold of a thick stem of the ivy that covered the wall of the house, and started to climb down.

'Easy does it!' Asb screeched suddenly.

'Whaaa —?' I lost my footing and found myself hanging by my fingertips from the ivy stem.

'Let your fingers do the walking,' coached the alien from hell.

'OhGodohGodohGod ...' I prayed, trying to strengthen my grip on the ivy stem.

'It's not too late, Alan,' declared Asb generously. 'You can still walk away from this.'

Walk away from this? Drop to my death, maybe, but not walk. I was about to say something harsh when, suddenly, the ivy stem began to come loose from the wall.

'Uh?' was all I could manage.

Then the ivy stem, with me firmly holding on to it, detached itself from the wall like some kind of giant green zipper and retraced its years of growth in about three seconds flat.

I was too terrified to scream, so my mouth was — thankfully, very thankfully — closed when I landed in Dad's compost heap.

'A soft landing!' grinned Asb, as I schlocked and glunched my way out of the cocktail of rotten grass cuttings, potato peelings, kitchen waste — and, oh yesss, horse manure — which was my father's compost heap.

There was no way I could get back into the house to clean myself up. Is it possible to strangle an avocado-shaped alien? I gave this question serious thought as I tried to wipe off the ... well, cleaned myself up as best I could.

Asb kept a safe distance from me as we made our way to the gardening festival. It must have read my thoughts. Well, maybe that was the reason.

We were fairly near the hall before we spotted anybody else.

'Quick! Hop into the bag!' I hissed.

It was time to put the plan into action.

*

When we got to the hall, everybody seemed keen on keeping their distance from me. The compost heap had left its mark. It seemed like every fly in town had fallen in love with me. They were hovering in a cloud over my head.

The people at the desk hardly said a word as I explained that I was the A. Murray who had entered the competition several weeks before. (My dad is called Alec.) Eyes watered as I was waved on. We were in!

'Whatever about looking the part, there is really no need to *smell* it!' sniffed a large lady in a floral hat, as she hauled a basket of oversized tomatoes onto a table.

'You need a powder that cleans the dirt that other powders leave behind,' preached a small voice from my shopping bag.

'You need to shut up!' I snapped at Asb. The large lady with the hat and the tomatoes didn't realise I was talking to the bag; she stormed off in a huff.

'Just sit here,' I hissed, hauling Asb out of the bag and wedging it between an outsized cauliflower and some Brussels sprouts that could have passed for cabbages.

'I'm surrounded by vegetables!' it said indignantly.

'Pull in your stalks and don't move!'

'Okay,' it muttered, subdued.

The judge was about ninety-seven. She moved at a snail's pace around stands laden with serious-looking vegetables — turnips with thunderous torsos, carrots that could fell a grown man, cabbages fit for kings, broccoli that you wouldn't want to mess with. Competitors milled around her, catching her elbow and jostling her walking-frame as they tried to draw her attention to their own home-grown miracles

I stood back. The only ones keeping me company were the flies.

'Huh!' the old lady grunted, prodding a cabbage. 'I wouldn't feed that to pigs.'

'Hah!' she wheezed, squeezing the oversized tomatoes. 'I wouldn't even use 'em for ketchup.'

'Hey!' she beamed, poking Asb and peering at its knobbly purple-green skin. 'I wouldn't say no to *that*!' She looked around at the eager faces. 'Whose is this?'

I took a step forward. The flies followed.

The judge eyed me up and down.

'So,' she said, 'what's your secret, kid?'

Then she paused and sniffed. Her nose wrinkled.

'Never mind,' she gasped. 'I think I can guess.'

The other contestants looked daggers at me. Old Floral-Hat-and-Tomatoes looked ready to scream.

*

The cup had 'A. Murray — Overall Winner' engraved on it. The cheque had the words 'one hundred' scribbled on it.

I took my trophy, my cheque and my, um, avocado, and high-tailed it out of there. I figured I'd give the trophy to Dad, someday. And as for the cheque ...

'We're in the money!' sang Asb from the shopping bag. 'It's a rich man's world!'

The man in the hardware shop was very kind. The three-hundred-litre deluxe bin, the double set of Santa Claus lights and the bumper container of Super Sudz (the powder that cleanz) actually cost £103.95, but he let me off with the straight hundred. Maybe he was in a good mood.

Maybe it was the smell — his eyes watered as I left the shop with my purchases. Maybe he just liked kids. Whatever it was, Asb was going home ... and none too soon for me!

Yet, that evening, as I held the lid open for Asb to climb into the bin, I felt a pang of sadness.

Would I ever see the little alien again? Was this the end?

'Never say never,' chirped Asb, giving me a high five (well, a high six, actually). 'I will be back. Do not adjust your set.'

Asb's eye-stalks tilted to gaze admiringly at the shiny new bin, which was studded with Christmas lights and stank of washing powder.

'Check this *out*! Beam me up, Scotty!'

The lid clanked shut, and I stood back to let the shiny three-hundred-litre dustbin hurtle into the night sky. Its little Santa lights flashed, and I watched them for a long time, until I could no longer make them out from the stars and the satellites and the pieces of space junk that orbit our great Earth.

El Kid

AISLINN O'LOUGHLIN

Parents!

Luke Reilly hated parents. He hated teachers, too, and school-bus drivers. And dinner ladies and caretakers and sports coaches and those guys who came in once a year to take school photographs. He also hated shop-owners, dentists, airline pilots, TV presenters, the president and — well, basically anyone old enough to be considered a grown-up.

Just because they were older, they thought they had some automatic right to boss kids around. 'Do your homework!' 'Pick that up and put it in the bin.' 'Stop hitting him!' 'No, you can't shower with your clothes on, I don't care how cold the bathroom is.' 'Take that cat out of the microwave … now!'

It drove Luke crazy. He was ten years old, for crying out loud; if he couldn't make his own decisions by now, he'd never be able to. He just wanted some way to make *them* do what *he* wanted for a change.

That was where the helmet came in useful.

*

Luke found the helmet one day in October, after a particularly nasty row with his teacher over why kids couldn't choose their own homework. The teacher got pretty worked up, and in the end Luke stormed out of the room and went for a long walk in the woods. Of course, his parents would go spare when they found out, but who cared?

He was walking along, trying to think up some way to make grown-ups take him seriously for a change, when he fell over something and landed flat on his face in a puddle.

'Ow!' he muttered, picking himself up. 'What the ...'

His voice trailed off as he saw what he'd tripped over.

It was black — at least, it looked black, but where the sun bounced off it Luke noticed a green shine. When he looked more closely, he realised that it was only the corner of something — probably something a lot bigger — which was buried under the mud.

He grabbed a pointy stone from nearby and began digging.

The ground was soft and slimy with mud. For once, Luke was actually glad of Irish weather. If it hadn't been for all the rain that everyone complained about, the ground would have been practically undiggable.

It still took him about an hour to uncover the thing, but it was well worth it.

'Wow,' Luke muttered, wiping it with the sleeve of his school shirt. 'It's a helmet! How cool is that?'

He held it up and grinned.

A real helmet! And not like any he'd ever seen before. This one was huge, with two holes at the top and huge round gaps for the eyes. Inside the helmet, Luke could feel a little bulge on either side, about where your temples would be when you put it on.

Was it worth anything? he wondered. After all, who knew how old it was? Maybe Viking invaders had lost it ... maybe it'd belonged to a Celtic warrior ... It was probably worth loads!

He glanced down at his watch. Three o'clock; school was over. Maybe he'd get lucky. Maybe the headmistress hadn't phoned his parents. He wasn't in the mood for a lecture on 'The Importance of Education in the Lives of Young People Today'. Not that he was ever in the mood for a lecture; but today he just wanted to lock himself in his room, clean up that helmet, and take a good look at it.

*

No such luck, unfortunately. The minute Luke stepped in the door, his mother dragged him into the sitting-room for a 'little talk'. He was glad he'd hidden the helmet in his bag (the fact that he'd had to dump most of his school-books was an added bonus). It would have been just like his mam to take it away, as a punishment or something.

As it was, there was only really one punishment she could give him. After Luke had spent about half an hour looking apologetic and mumbling 'I'm sorry' and 'I know' and 'I won't do it again', his mam said just what he'd been hoping she would.

'Luke, go to your room!'
'But, Mam —' he began.
'Now, Luke.'
'But —'
'Go!'
'Oh, all right,' he sighed.

He trudged up the stairs, clutching his bag, trying to make his back look as pitiful as possible in case his mam was still watching, and smiling to himself. He dodged into the bathroom for a second, to grab a basin of water, an old toothbrush and a couple of J-cloths, before locking himself in his room.

He sat down on the side of his bed and lifted the helmet carefully out of his bag.

'Now let's have a real look at you,' he whispered.

*

Luke caught his breath in awe as he held the spotless, gleaming helmet up to the light and watched the whole spectrum of colours dance across the rim.

And if it hadn't been for Mrs Carter's bad temper, he thought, easing the helmet onto his head, *I might never have found it. Maybe adults do have their uses after all. I'd still like to give them a taste of their own medicine, though.*

SO DO IT, boomed a voice.

Luke jumped and glanced around.

'Who —' he began.

DO IT, said the voice again. SHOW THEM WHAT IT'S LIKE TO BE TOLD WHAT TO DO ALL THE TIME.

Luke looked around the room nervously and lifted the helmet from his head. 'Where are you?' he demanded.

Silence.

'Where are you?' he repeated.

Suddenly, a thought struck him. He put the helmet on again.

Hello? he thought.

HELLO, LUKE, said the voice.

Who are you? asked Luke. *What the hell is going on?*

DOES IT REALLY MATTER? asked the helmet. I CAN TELL YOU HOW TO OVERTHROW ADULTS ONCE AND FOR ALL. JUST THINK OF IT, LUKE — A WORLD RUN BY KIDS. ADULTS WOULD BE NOTHING MORE THAN SLAVES, OBEYING YOUR EVERY COMMAND, CATERING TO YOUR EVERY WHIM. AND YOU, LUKE REILLY, WOULD REAP THE BENEFITS THAT COME WITH BEING A REVOLUTIONARY LEADER. YOU WOULD REIGN SUPREME, OVER KIDS AND ADULTS, KING OF THE WORLD. YOU WOULD BE … EL KID!

El Kid, thought Luke. *King of the World. I like it. But — overthrow the adults? Lead a kids' revolution and win? Nobody could do that. You're crazy.*

CRAZY, LUKE? said the helmet. YOU'RE THE ONE TALKING TO A HELMET. LOOK, IF YOU WANT TO DO THIS, I CAN GIVE YOU ALL THE INFORMATION YOU NEED. I CAN SHOW YOU HOW TO BUILD A WEAPON THAT NOBODY COULD OVERCOME. IF YOU BUILD IT, THEY WILL LOSE. WITH THE HELP OF OTHER KIDS, YOU COULD HAVE IT READY IN A COUPLE OF MONTHS.

If I build it, they will lose? repeated Luke. *But are you sure I could get other kids to help?*

ANY KID WHO'S EVER HAD HIS POCKET MONEY CANCELLED BY AN UNREASONABLE PARENT WILL JUMP AT THE CHANCE, the helmet assured him. ESPECIALLY ONCE YOU'VE FINISHED YOUR TRAINING.

*

A talking helmet can do some strange things, as Luke spent the rest of the night finding out. First, it decided that Luke needed a crash course in leadership skills. This course lasted sixty-seven seconds, and consisted of huge stores of information being passed almost directly to Luke's brain from the helmet, through those little bulges he'd felt on the inside. Then it gave him a thirty-second course on tactics and negotiating, which jammed his brain with the kind of information most army generals would kill for. It told him about the great leaders of history — how they built up their successes and empires, and how to avoid the mistakes which (in many cases) caused their downfall. In thirty-five seconds Luke learned everything he needed to know about propaganda, image and charisma — or, as the helmet called it, 'Forty-Seven Thousand Steps to Becoming the Most Popular Kid in the Universe'.

And then came the fun part: a forty-five-minute session which taught Luke everything he needed to know in order to build the most amazing weapon on Earth. His mind was bombarded by pictures, measurements, references to electrical equipment he hadn't even known existed, and more acronyms than he'd ever imagined.

Whoa, thought Luke with a gasp, collapsing back onto his bed as the helmet finished his training. *I understand technobabble. Even more than most ten-year-olds do.*

THAT'S RIGHT, said the helmet. BUT REMEMBER — IF YOU DON'T KEEP UP YOUR TRAINING, IF YOU DON'T REFRESH YOUR MEMORY EVERY DAY, THAT INFORMATION WILL FADE. YOU'LL BE BACK TO BEING JUST ANOTHER KID. AND YOU DON'T WANT THAT, DO YOU, LUKE?

Heck, no, said Luke. *I'm the smartest kid on the planet! I'm probably the smartest person on the planet!*

AND YOU'VE GOT A LONG DAY AHEAD OF YOU TOMORROW, said the helmet. SO TAKE ME OFF AND GET SOME SLEEP. IT'LL HELP YOUR BRAIN PROCESS ALL THAT INFORMATION.

Okay, Dad, grinned Luke, lifting the helmet from his head. *G'night.*

GOOD NIGHT, LUKE, said the helmet.

Then, when it knew Luke couldn't hear it any more, it added: SUCKER!

*

School the next day was — well, it was an experience.

Luke had never had any trouble convincing people to do things. He didn't have problems with confidence (even if he had, the helmet's training would have got rid of them pretty quickly); and his mates were the kind of people nobody argues with. But this was different. This time he had to convince people that they wanted to do something, not just for the good of their health, but for the good of humanity.

His friends were easy enough to convince; he'd sold them on the idea of getting even with adults years before. Now that he actually knew how to do it, they were only too willing to help.

The next step was more difficult. Obviously, making a speech to the entire school in the middle of the playground was out of the question. Instead, Luke gathered together the most popular kids from each class, a year at a time, and talked to them quietly about his ideas.

'I mean, look what they're doing,' he insisted, to the sixth-classers. 'Burning holes in the ozone layer, starting huge wars on any excuse, and then claiming to be mature. Most of us don't hold grudges for more than a few days; their grudges can last hundreds of years. Look at us — we don't care about skin colour or religion or social differences or anything like that. As long as you're nice to me, I'll be nice to you, am I right?

'And has anyone ever noticed how many times some criminal on telly gets away with something, or gets a light sentence, 'cause of the way he was brought up? The way he was brought up, friends! The lousy job our parents do on us can affect us for the rest of our lives! We could become lousy grown-ups, just because our parents were!

'Writers are always going on about kids' idyllic world, and how growing up can lose us that world. Well, I say it's time to stop living in this dysfunctional planet the grown-ups have created. It's time to spread the idyllic world of the child across the planet! Are you with me?'

The twelve-year-olds in front of him shuffled their feet and stared at the ground.

'I said,' repeated Luke, 'are you with me?'

'But I like my parents,' muttered a girl. 'I don't want to overthrow them.'

'Well, of course you like your parents,' said Luke, 'but you've got to think about the good of the planet, not just about what suits you. Is it worth it — to let the grown-ups keep hating and killing and destroying the planet, just because you like your parents? Don't you think you deserve better than the messed-up world your parents are helping to uphold?'

'Guess so,' said the girl.

'Then isn't it worth it — to make a few little sacrifices so we can create a new world?'

'Well, yeah,' said the girl.

'So are you with me?'

'Yeah,' said the girl.

'Then say it louder!'

'Yeah!' she yelled.

'Louder!'

'Yeah!' she screamed.

'You're all with me, aren't you?' cried Luke.

'YEAH!' shrieked the sixth-classers.

'Then let's hear it for El Kid!' shouted Bobby Kelly, Luke's best friend. 'El Kid, El Kid, El Kid …'

'El Kid, El Kid …' chanted the group.

'Then go spread the word to your friends!' cried Luke. The older kids left, still chanting his name.

'Wow!' gasped Bobby. 'How did you do that? All that stuff about the id … idal … the world of the kid and stuff. I mean, did you mean it?'

'Heck, no,' said Luke. 'I just wanna take over the world. It's what's called catering for the audience, Bobby. Twelve-year-olds want something that sounds intelligent, so you give 'em long words and talk about peace and harmony.'

A sudden cough from behind made him turn around.

'Lu — er, El Kid, *sir!*' said Dave Johnson, snapping to attention. 'I got the senior infants here for ya.'

Luke looked at the group of five-year-olds in front of him.

'Right, kids!' he grinned. 'Who wants free ice-cream?'

By the end of the day, everyone in the school had heard about El Kid's plan to overthrow the adults — and they liked it. They developed their own private salute (slap your bum, slap your head, slap your chest and wave). They went home and spread the word to the other kids on their streets, kids who went to different schools. *They* spread the word around *their* schools. The kids in the area held meetings after school, and soon kids in other areas were doing the same. Some of the more computer-literate ones set up 'El Kid' websites and mailing lists, and soon kids in other countries were hearing Luke's ideas.

They were all sworn to secrecy against telling adults, but they could tell their mates — who told their mates, who told *their* mates. Within a few months, millions of kids all over the planet were pledging allegiance to El Kid.

*

This is really happening, isn't it? Luke said one day, as he lay on his bed after his re-training session. It was December, just a few days before Christmas.

WAS THERE EVER ANY DOUBT? asked the helmet. I MEAN, LOOK WHO YOU HAD FOR YOUR MENTOR! SO HOW'S THE BUG GOING?

Nearly finished, said Luke.

'The Bug' was the name Luke had given the revolutionary weapon that the helmet had taught him about. It was something like a plane, but not all that much. Luke hadn't realised this until he'd started to draw the plans, but it was shaped like a giant bug, with huge eye-like windows in front and two antennae sticking out of its head.

Unlike other insects, however, Luke's Bug could do more with its antennae than just feel around for things. At the tip of each antenna was a small sensor, sensitive to light, heat, sound, movement and just about anything else that could give away where someone was. It could locate its target from miles away. Inside the antennae were tiny lasers, so accurate they could shoot fleas on a dog's back without the dog even noticing (Luke knew this for a fact; his dog had never noticed). But it wasn't fleas that Luke was interested in shooting.

ANY RESISTANCE FROM THE ADULTS, the helmet had told him, CAN EASILY BE QUELLED BY THE BUG. WHO WOULD DARE ARGUE WITH YOU, ONCE THEY KNOW THAT YOU COULD BE ANYWHERE ON THE PLANET IN UNDER HALF A MINUTE, AND THAT IT WOULDN'T TAKE YOU MUCH LONGER TO HAVE THEM LOCATED AND EXECUTED?

You mean I get to frizzle some grown-ups? grinned Luke.

AS MANY AS YOU WANT, said the helmet, ANYWHERE YOU WANT.

As far as the Bug was concerned, the speed of light was for other, slower forms of transport. The Bug was built to do battle, at any time, in any place — or in several places, almost simultaneously, if the need arose.

*

'Are you sure this is going to work, El Kid, *sir*?' asked Bobby, as they prepared to make their existence known to the adult world.

'What — you think I can build the most powerful fighter-ship the world has ever seen, but I can't hack into a few hundred TV studios and hook up a simple video-link?' said Luke.

'Not actually what I was talking about …' said Bobby. Then, noticing the look that Luke was giving him, he straightened up and added, 'But I trust in your genius, El Kid, *sir*!'

'As you should,' said Luke.

They were sitting in one of the cabins they'd built in the woods, near where they were keeping the Bug. The kids figured that, once the revolution started, it wouldn't be a very smart move to keep living at home with their parents. All around the world, children had been building huts to share during the rebellion. Obviously, afterwards, when the adults had been reduced to slave status, the kids would be able to move back to their own houses; but until then, this was safer.

'And you're on in three … two … one …' said Dave, activating the transmitter.

All over the planet, television screens fuzzed and blurred. Suddenly, the image of a small blond boy with a serious face replaced dinnertime soaps, breakfast shows and late-night movies.

Adults watched, transfixed, as Luke began to speak.

'Adults of the world,' he said, 'your reign has ended. No longer will children live by your rules. Tomorrow night, at midnight, a new millennium will dawn, and with it a new era — the Era of the Kid. As I speak, millions of children all around the world are preparing to overthrow adultkind, by force if necessary. You cannot win. We may be small, but we've got you outnumbered!

'If you think I'm bluffing, ask yourselves this: where are your kids right now? Not in the room with you, I'll bet. Not in their beds. Not at home at all. They're out, just like every other kid, preparing to fight for a world where children have the right to do whatever the heck we want!

'And don't think your armies can beat us. We have a secret weapon, so fast and so powerful that no weapon known to mankind — I mean, to *adult*kind — can destroy it!

'Our representatives around the world will be contacting your leaders. You have until midnight tomorrow to surrender the planet to us. If you don't, we will wage war against adultkind, driving you to destruction if we must! Peace or war — it is in your hands. El Kid has spoken!'

The message ended, and television shows resumed as normal. Not that it mattered. The adults of the world were too stunned by what they had just seen to think about *Neighbours* or *Oprah*.

*

Within half an hour, the phone line which Luke had hooked up in his cabin began to hop with calls from El Kid reps all over the world.

'President Clinton wants a conference link-up ...'

'The Queen wants to talk to you, and Mr Blair wants a video conference ...'

'Boris Yeltsin is demanding a meeting ...'

This suited Luke just fine. He wanted a chance to let the world leaders see exactly what his new toy could do.

A video link-up, he decided, would work quite nicely.

*

Through their video screens, the adults gaped in horror at the pile of ash which, just a millisecond earlier, had been a huge oak tree.

'Are we convinced yet, grown-ups?' asked Luke. 'Or would we like to see a demonstration on a human subject? I can do far more damage than this. Perhaps you *would* like to see how quickly I can seek and destroy a grown-up target, hmm?'

Luke climbed into the Bug again and took off. Almost instantly, the delegates gasped in shock as a straight bald line suddenly ran from Bill Clinton's forehead to the nape of his neck.

'What?' asked Clinton. Somebody handed him a mirror. Luke landed just in time to see the president's eyes stretch wide with fear.

'Oh, dear Lord, that thing's real! Would you look at what that brat's done to my hair?'

El Kid grinned.

'Ladies and gentlemen, you have until midnight tomorrow!'

*

Luke didn't usually read papers or watch the news, but the next day he was glued to both. Story after story reported on the kid who was threatening the planet and had left adults helpless.

The adults didn't seem to think there was much they could do. The thought of fighting their own kids disgusted them so much that most refused to even consider a war.

This left them with only one option.

*

Wow, said Luke, as he sat on the floor of his cabin, *in a few minutes I'm gonna rule the world! This rocks! I ... Hang on a second.*

He paused to brush away a few creepy-crawlies that were climbing up his leg.

I'm gonna be king! he continued. *I'm ...* He stopped again. *Oh, man, this place is crawling with bugs. Don't you just hate them?*

Um, said the helmet.

Listen, thanks for the brain-boost, said Luke, *but I've gotta get outside. It's time for my link-up.*

Listen, Luke, said the helmet, I've —

Whatever it is, said Luke, taking the helmet off, *I'm sure it can wait till I'm ruling the world.*

He stood up and looked around. The floor was

absolutely covered with bugs!

Luke pushed the window open. 'Thank heavens for the miracles of architecture,' he said to himself, hopping onto the windowsill. 'No way the King of the World should have to walk through all that!'

*

'You ready, El Kid, *sir*?' asked Dave, focusing the camera on Luke and flicking a bug off the lens. 'Darn it! Where are all these bugs coming from?'

Luke gave him a look. 'We're about to take over the world, and you're thinking about a few bugs? You worry me, Johnson.' He glanced behind him at the only Bug that mattered, making sure that it was just far enough from him to be seen fully on camera without looking too small.

'You're on, *sir*!' replied Dave.

Luke glanced around at the screens. The worried faces of the world leaders looked back at him. Clinton was wearing a hat.

'Well,' said El Kid, 'have we reached a decision, grown-ups?'

'El Kid,' said Clinton, 'the adults of the world are unwilling to fight our own children. Your little display yesterday has proved that you are more than a match for us, and it is for that reason — Oh dear Lord, what is *that*?'

He gasped and pointed. 'Behind you, Kid! What the heck is going on?'

El Kid giggled.

'Nice try, but it's a bit late for distraction techniques now,' he said.

'No, Luke, he's serious!' shrieked Bobby. 'Look behind you!'

Luke spun around, and screamed.

In front of him, swarms of bugs — there must have been millions of them — were forming themselves into what looked like huge pillars. Luke and the world leaders stared in horror as the pillars began to melt and fuse, until they were no longer heaps of separate insects, but seven solid blocks. Then, slowly, these masses began to take shape, developing heads, and legs ... and antennae.

Luke realised that what was standing in front of him was a troop of giant bugs. One of them was holding his helmet.

'Who ...' began Luke, turning white. 'What ... what ...'

The bug with the helmet stepped forward.

'Luke,' he said, 'I am TuNinChee. I must thank you for rebuilding our ship. When we crashed here, a thousand Earth-years ago, we weren't sure we would ever make it home. We had lost our information helmet. We were trapped.

'In order not to draw attention to ourselves, we disjointed — broke our bodies into little pieces resembling your Earth insects. We had just located our helmet and begun to push it to the surface of the earth when you found it. One of JyKonNix's disjointed parts was still inside the helmet.'

Luke gave a half-smile of disbelief as one of the giant bugs waved at him.

'He saw your desire to overthrow the adults as a way to get our ship rebuilt. It was he who communicated with you. He passed on some information — the information relating to Earth leaders and tactics — to the helmet, which combined it with already-stored knowledge to give you your crash courses.

'Your television appearance yesterday was a signal to the rest of us that the ship was ready.'

'I'm sorry, Luke,' JyKonNix said.

He glanced at the bewildered faces of the world leaders. 'Don't worry,' he said. 'In a couple of days he won't remember anything I've taught him. I hope this doesn't affect intergalactic relations in the future. But now we've got to fly. They'll be wondering what's keeping us, back home.'

TuNinChee placed the helmet over his head, his antennae sticking out through the holes at the top.

'I hope we can visit again,' he said, 'under less … confusing circumstances.'

With that, the troop boarded the Bug and took off.

Luke was left staring up into space, watching his dream disappear into the stars.

'I hate bugs!' he muttered.

The Survivor

LARRY O'LOUGHLIN

Crocker grunted as he struggled up the beach, dragging the last sheet of corrugated-iron fencing. His body was covered in sweat, and blue veins bulged at his temples. He stopped and turned his head. The rest of the fencing was just a few paces further. It might as well have been miles away. He was gasping for breath, and his shoulders were straining until he was convinced that the slightest jolt would snap them clean out of their sockets.

'Stuff it! Close enough.'

He dropped the fencing and lowered himself, slowly and carefully, onto the sand. He reached towards his shorts pocket and winced; after four hours of physical effort, even that hurt. He felt like brain-dead Lenny's joke: 'I got aches in places where I didn't even know I got places.'

He'd forgotten how painful physical work

could be. *Hell, when did I ever know?* He hadn't done any physical work since childhood. He didn't have to. Muscle wasn't his department; that was for Lenny. Crocker was a Brain, a planner.

That was how his world was divided: into two neat little boxes, one marked 'Muscle', the other marked 'Brain'. There was a third box — the one marked 'Victim' — but no one really cared about that one.

Crocker could easily have been a Victim. After his first schoolyard beating, when he'd realised that a small chubby body wasn't designed for either fighting or fleeing, it could have gone either way — Victim or Brain.

That was when he'd noticed Lenny. Big, strong, loner Lenny, always the outsider, always the one looking on.

So Crocker had played a hunch.

'You know those two kids who jumped me?'

'Yeah.'

'I reckon you could take 'em with one hand behind your back.'

'Why should I?'

''Cause I'll give you three bars of chocolate if you do.'

The hunch had worked. Lenny's justice was swift and effective. After that, no one had ever laid a finger on Crocker again.

But what had really made Crocker a Brain wasn't just the beating. It was spotting the opportunity to take it one step further. That was why he'd gone back and taken the two kids' lunch money while they were on the ground, and why, later, he'd gone back again to suggest that if they didn't want another beating they'd better hand over their lunch money *every* day.

It had been the start of a meaningful and profitable relationship. Crocker and Lenny had graduated from schoolyard hoods to men with a finger in every racket going.

Muscle, Brain and Victim — Crocker's holy trinity.

He pushed himself up to a sitting position, pulled out his cigarettes and lighter, lit a cigarette. In the moonlight he could see the long scar in the sand where he'd hauled the fencing up the beach, one piece at a time. Lenny'd have done it in a twentieth of the time, he knew that. *Hell, that dumb-ass would probably have carried the whole lot, boat and all, at one go.*

But he didn't want Lenny on this job. He didn't even want Lenny to know about it. This was different. It wasn't business. It was personal.

He watched as the boat that had brought him to the island bobbed about near the shore. He checked his watch: 12.01 am. He reached down and turned on the small battery-operated radio clipped to his shorts.

'… And that was the theme from the movie *A Bug's Life*,' intoned an over-enthusiastic DJ, as some song began to fade, 'bringing us into the last day of the millennium. Get it? *A Bug's Life?*'

Crocker got it.

'Just twenty-three hours and fifty-nine minutes away from the Big One. So let's kick off with another appropriate little ditty — this time it's "I Will Survive" …'

Crocker switched off the radio.

Like the dance band on the Titanic, he thought derisively. Somewhere, he didn't know where, he'd heard that the dance band on the *Titanic* had kept playing as the boat sank. *Bunch of dumb-asses.* If he'd been there, he'd have been selling seats on the lifeboats while Lenny raided the bar.

Lenny.

It was Lenny who had given Crocker the idea, the year before.

*

'Hey, boss. Why don't we do something about this bug thing?'

'What bug thing?'

'You know, the bug that's going to eat all the computers and put us all in deep shit next New Year's Day. We'd make a fortune if we could invent a bug spray.'

That had been in February 1998. It was the first time Crocker had heard of the millennium bug. Over the next few months it was mentioned in every paper and every TV news program he saw.

Lenny had got it wrong, as usual, but not completely. The millennium bug wasn't an insect; it was an oversight, a design fault, that meant that the world's computers weren't going to be able to handle the date '2000'. At one second past midnight on 1 January 2000, they'd crash, throwing everything into chaos. The banks, the stock markets, the airlines, communications, the water and power supplies — everything. The whole world would grind to a halt as things went into gridlock on a global scale.

Lenny was right: there was money to be made.

After the crash would come the chaos. Stock markets and bank records would be wiped out; personal fortunes would just disappear, reducing thousands of people to paupers overnight. All the utilities — water, gas, electricity — would just cease to function. There'd be food shortages caused by panic buying and delivery failures. As a result, there'd be looting and rioting, practically civil war, in all the major cities. Armed mobs and gangs would roam the streets, attacking whoever and whatever they wanted. There'd be armed battles as the armies and police forces came face to face with the rioters. Hundreds of thousands of people would die. No one and nothing would be safe.

Then, slowly, things would start to settle down, as governments and armies regained control of the streets and utilities and food supplies were gradually restored.

Crocker had no idea how long the chaos would last. Two weeks, a month, two months? He didn't know and he didn't care. But if he was right — and he was sure he was — then, when it all settled down, there'd be millions to be made. There'd be thousands and thousands of newly poor people lining the streets, selling everything they owned — jewels, homes, businesses — just to survive. There'd be the rebuilding program, needing supplies and equipment at any price. There'd be … He could only guess at how many other money-making opportunities there'd be. It would be glorious.

And to cash in, all you had to do was survive and have money. He intended to do both.

Everything he'd done over the last few months had been done to ensure that, whoever else was destroyed in the chaos, he would survive. To do that, he needed just two things: absolute secrecy and someplace safe to stay.

The first part was easy. He told no one about his plans, not even Lenny.

The second part was where the island came in.

He'd noticed it on one of their mid-ocean rendezvous with the ships bringing in illegal immigrants at a thousand bucks per head — Crocker always insisted on being paid in American dollars. You always knew where you were with dollars. *Trust the almighty dollar. Sixty thousand international criminals can't be wrong.*

He'd seen the island's potential immediately. It was off the main shipping lanes and flight paths, far enough from the mainland to be isolated, and small enough to be easily defended against any other would-be survivors who might stray his way.

Tracing the owners, a couple of old women living in a nursing home, hadn't been difficult; but persuading them to sell had turned out to be much harder than he'd expected. He'd thought cash would do it, so he'd raised his offer twice. But they just didn't want to let it go. It had 'sentimental value' to them. *Sentimental value? Yeah, sure.*

In the end, Lenny had been sent in to persuade them. As usual, he had been very persuasive — even if he hadn't known exactly what he was persuading them to do.

*

Crocker watched the boat for another couple of minutes. Then he pushed himself up and walked down to the water. He reached into the boat, took out a can of petrol, unscrewed the cap and tossed it onto the sand. Walking the length of the boat, he poured the petrol all over it.

He leaned over and turned the ignition key, and the engine came alive. He nudged the boat gently away from the shore. The wheel was already tied in a fixed position, so the boat would go straight out onto the open sea. As it moved away, he flicked what was left of his cigarette on board. Within seconds the boat was ablaze.

Crocker watched it go. It blazed for a few minutes, then slowly disappeared under the waves. There was no explosion to attract attention. He'd drained the tanks, leaving just enough to get the boat started, to ensure that there wouldn't be.

*

He walked over to the small brush-covered shed, opened the door and flicked on the battery-operated light. He'd been doing midnight runs to the island for a couple of months, and everything he needed to ensure his survival was right there. A small camp-bed and a bedroll were tucked into a corner. Stacked neatly on pallets beside them were hundreds of jumbo-sized tins of meat, vegetables, condensed milk, fruit, fruit juice and water biscuits, all liberated from aid ships carrying them to wherever the latest famine happened to be. Piled against the far wall were four hundred two-litre containers of water; they'd been salvaged from a supply truck that had gone missing from a truck stop. In front of them were medical supplies, stoves and utensils, bought at a knockdown price from the quartermaster at the local army base.

May he rot in hell, the swindling swine.

The sergeant, after agreeing to supply Crocker with enough weapons and ammunition to arm a fair-sized raiding party, had had the nerve to try and raise the price. He'd received his payment, but he hadn't lived long enough to enjoy it; two days later, he'd been found in an alleyway with his neck broken.

The radio and the tool kit had been bought from a store, at full price. *Some you win, some you lose.*

Crocker reached under the bed and pulled out six metal briefcases, one by one. There was no need to check them — he'd only just brought them to the island — but he checked anyway, opening each case in turn. He gazed lovingly at the banknotes. One million, in hundreds and thousands, in each case: six million bucks in total. Everything he'd raised in his thirty-year career. He'd changed it all into American dollars; he figured that was the only currency that would still be accepted and valuable all over the world, after the meltdown.

He closed the cases, put them back under the bed, and picked up the tool kit.

Time to go to work.

*

By 10.00 am the island had been transformed into a small fortress, completely encased in a corrugated iron fence. Crocker had been building the fence for a couple of months, a little each week; the sheets he'd brought in on this last trip had completed the job.

The whole shoreline outside the fence was mined; there were land-mines every few feet, and he'd mapped the exact location of each one. A second ring of mines, half-submerged and held in place by a cordon of chains, encircled the island, just feet from the shore. He'd settled machine-gun emplacements at various points along the corrugated encasement. In the centre of the compound was a small battery of rocket-launchers and flamethrowers. All the weaponry was primed and ready for use.

Crocker wasn't much of a military man, but he reckoned he had enough hardware to keep any unwelcome visitors at bay. Let them have their civil war. He'd pick up the pieces when it was all over.

He sat down on the crate that held the inflatable which would take him back to the mainland when the time came, and rested his feet on a case of ammunition. He lifted a can of beer, pulled off the tab and raised it to his lips.

'A toast,' he said, to the fence. 'To me, Jim Crocker — a survivor.'

He finished his beer, went into the shed and crawled into his camp-bed. He was asleep in seconds.

*

Lenny checked the time again. 11.28 p.m. The Boss was never late, never. Not until now.

He thought back to their conversation the previous night.

'Listen, Lenny, I've got a couple of things I gotta do. I'm gonna have to take the boat out. I'll meet you tomorrow, my place, 11.15. If I'm not there, go on to the party without me.'

He couldn't do that. He couldn't go without the Boss. It would be no fun without his best friend.

He checked his watch again. 11.30.

There was definitely something up.

Lenny picked up the phone and anxiously punched in the number for the guard at the marina. After a brief conversation, he put the phone down. The boat wasn't there, and there was no sign of anything coming in.

He looked at his watch again. 11.32. Then he made a decision.

He picked up the car keys and left the flat. Taking the steps two at a time, he was down in the underground car park in seconds. He leaped into his car and headed for the small airfield at the edge of town. The car clock showed the time as 11.34.

*

Crocker woke up, looked at the luminous dial on the clock and pushed himself out of bed. 11.00 p.m. — one hour to gridlock. He turned on the radio. Some mindless idiot was babbling on about the biggest party in history and urging people to spare a thought for those who'd be spending the night on their own.

'Don't worry about me,' laughed Crocker, unscrewing the top of a bottle of ten-year-old malt whiskey. 'I'll be doing just fine out here.' *Shame about Lenny, though. I wonder if the dumb-ass has figured out I'm not coming yet.*

He raised the bottle to his lips.

'To absent friends,' he smiled.

*

'Look, mister, I don't know if there's enough fuel for another full sweep,' groaned the kid behind the wheel of the seaplane. 'We've already been up once. My dad only agreed to let us party in her if we swore we'd take her up for no more than ten minutes. So that's all the fuel we have, and anyway the hydraulics are ...'

Lenny wasn't listening. He pointed his gun at the small blonde girl.

'Okay. Okay. Don't do anything silly,' said the kid, holding out the keys. 'Take it, Okay? We're cool.'

Lenny waved his gun, and the kids sprinted into the darkness. He climbed onto the plane and started the engines. He checked his watch. 11.57.

It had taken him twenty minutes to get to the airport. It would normally have taken five, but every asshole in the country seemed to be driving either into or out of town. Every few minutes he'd phoned the marina. Same story every time: no sign of Crocker.

He'd guessed there'd be some young rich kids at the airport, getting ready to bring in the new millennium by making a nuisance of themselves up in the air in Daddy's plane. He'd been right, but most had been too drunk even to stand. He'd found the girl and boy sitting on the steps of the seaplane, at the water's edge, drinking Coke and eating burritos.

He taxied out onto the bay, built up speed and lifted off smoothly.

*

Crocker sat on the packing-case listening to the countdown. The empty whiskey bottle was at his side and he was on his second beer. He didn't normally drink that much, but tonight was a special night. Tonight, he'd inherit the Earth.

Suddenly he thought of Lenny again. For a

second, just a second, he missed him, was sorry he'd lied to him, wished he'd brought him along. *What the hell. God knows what dumb chick Lenny would have ended up telling about the plan, if he'd known!* Lenny was expendable. There was plenty of muscle for hire, if you had the money. *Anyway, who knows? Lenny might survive the chaos.* If he did, they'd take up where they'd left off, and Lenny'd be none the wiser.

'Bye, you dumb klutz,' laughed Crocker, opening another beer. *All the same, I wouldn't mind seeing him one last time.*

The countdown on the radio was moving towards midnight. 'And now, with only thirty seconds to go ...' yelled the idiot announcer. In the background Crocker could hear laughter, music, excited screaming. *Party on, dumb-asses*, he thought. *Enjoy it while it lasts.*

He pulled a cigarette out of his pocket, lit up and inhaled deeply.

He was going to enjoy this.

*

Lenny circled the bay and the illegals' route for a third time. There was still no sign of the boat, and he was getting frantic. *The Boss must be in real trouble!*

He swept back over the little island they'd passed a couple of times. Maybe, just maybe, if the boat had got into trouble the Boss would have headed for there.

Still no sign ... Lenny turned for the mainland.

Then he saw the light. He banked the plane and brought her around.

'Gotcha, Boss. Gotcha.' He smiled.

*

'Ten! ... Nine! ... Eight!' screamed the announcer.

Crocker heard the plane and looked up. He lifted his night-vision glasses. He could see Lenny's face clearly.

'Seven!'

*

Lenny's smile faded as the engines spluttered and then stopped. The kid had warned him the fuel was almost gone. He'd have to try an emergency landing at sea and drift onto the beach.

Lenny tried to pull up, to land the plane gently, but she wasn't responding.

What was it the kid had said? The hydraulics ... *Damn!*

*

'Six!'

Crocker heard the change in the sound of the engine. He saw Lenny's face contort in fear and bewilderment as he fought to control the plane. She was coming in too fast. She was heading straight for the fence.

'Five! ... Four!'

'You dumb shit!' screamed Crocker. 'You dumb-ass —'

The plane hit the outer line of mines and burst into flames.

The momentum carried part of the flaming wreckage up the beach, onto the second line of mines. Crocker heard the explosions and watched in horror as pieces of burning wreckage were hurled though the fence, landing among the boxes of ammunition.

'... *One!*'

'You dumb bastard!' he screamed.

'*Zeroooo!*'

Then the island ignited like a Roman candle.

*

'And now, over to the newsroom. Good morning, and this is the news at midday on the first day of the new millennium. The thousands of computer workers hired to protect operating systems worldwide from the millennium bug seem to have succeeded in preventing the worst of the predicted effects. While many banks report minor losses of data, and a few airlines have had to cancel flights due to difficulties with scheduling computers, most systems seem to have made the transition with no serious problems. All utility services are still in place, except in areas around northern and southern France, so you'll be able to cook yourself a New Millennium Day dinner — if you're able for it after last night, that is!

'In local news, a plane-jacking turned into a

disaster last night, when the seaplane involved crashed into a small island off the west coast. Police who landed by helicopter found two bodies, too badly burned to be identifiable. There were no survivors.

'Apart from the crash, New Millennium Day passed uneventfully. No other deaths were reported locally. There were, however, a number of reports of minor injuries among revellers who …'

The Wishbone

MARK O'SULLIVAN

The day Dad left, we had chicken for dinner. Well, chicken was on the menu, but it ended up in the bin. The slash of his and Mam's words. The flash of the carving-knife. This is what I remember. And great, grainy gouges of white meat falling apart in a forlorn heap as he sliced.

When he came to pulling out the wishbone, I thought it would snap between his trembling fingers. He tossed the little Y-shaped bone aside and it fell on the floor. I knew then that I wouldn't be pulling the wishbone with him ever again.

I was seven years old. My wavy red hair reached almost to my waist, like the hair on the Barbie doll I was holding below the table-top. Before that, the arguments had always ended when one or the other of them — usually Mam — looked down at me and took pity. That

Sunday, I might as well not have been there. They didn't see me disappear from the table, pick up the wishbone and leave. They didn't see me. The Invisible Girl.

In my bedroom, I found a small blue velvet ring-box for the wishbone. I got a pair of scissors from the bathroom and cut my Barbie's long hair down to the plastic scalp. Then I waited for all the shouting to end, and it did.

*

For eight years I stay invisible, silent, anonymous. I don't argue, I do what I'm told at home, at school. Anything for a quiet life. And no one knows the real me. In Mam's pitying eyes, I'm the poor little girl betrayed by a cruel daddy. My every minute is organised and I'm never left alone. To Dad, I'm the pretty Barbie doll whose long hair he adores and who gets squeezed into his high-flying schedule two or three times a year. A weekend in Brussels here, a few days in Paris there; bags of Nike and Reebok gear to keep me happy until the next time.

All these years, I keep the wishbone and take it everywhere with me. The bone loses its moist cream colour, then its dry white, and turns grey, grows small. I wish my days away on it. Wish they'd get back together, wish he'd tire of his city-hopping life and she'd stop watching my every move. Wish, later, that she'd find someone or something to make her happy. Wish they'd see me, really see me. Wish someone, anyone, could see me.

Then, on my fifteenth birthday, something snaps in me. The wishing ends. I'm no longer invisible. At the end of that long day, the wishbone is broken.

*

Mam won't answer the phone because she knows it's him. He never forgets to ring on the morning of my birthday.

I should be grateful but I'm not. I've woken up in this weird mood. I'm sure something big is going to happen and I can't tell if it's good or bad, so I don't want the day to start.

I let the phone ring on and she shouts up the stairs. I'm wishing she'd just pick up the phone and have a civilised conversation with him. In the end, I give up and go down.

His voice sounds close but I'm miles away.

'How's my little birthday girl?'

'Fine.'

'Any plans for today? Any wild parties?'

'No,' I answer. Then I try a bit harder, like a good girl should. 'I've school; that's about all.'

'The new school's okay, is it?'

'Yeah,' I lie. It's a dive, just like the rest of this town we moved to a few months ago, when Mam got promoted in the bank.

'Bet you've lots of friends already.'

'Sort of.'

The conversation drags on. He tells me where he is — Geneva. I hear all about the deal he's working on, the problems, all that business stuff that makes him happy. He says there's a cheque in the post for me and I thank him.

'And, listen, I'll be in Budapest next month,' he adds. 'How would you fancy a weekend there?'

'That'd be … cool.'

I put the phone down and wish I still had a Barbie and a pair of bloody sharp scissors.

*

It's true I don't have any plans for my birthday, but Mam has. As she drives me to school, she goes through the arrangements. I nod, chip in a few 'yeah's, and look out at the grey day and the town that's already boringly familiar. In the pocket of my green school blazer my fist is filled with the velvet ring-box. If I squeeze a little harder, it'll break. The wishbone too. I stop myself.

Since we came to this town, I've been seeing less of Mam. She's an assistant manager now and she often has to work late, even go away overnight for conferences and stuff. Still, my life is no freer. She's got friendly with the people next door, the Hanleys, and that's where I spend the time when Mam's not home. They're an okay family except for the eldest, Caroline, who's my age. According to Mam and Mrs Hanley, we're best friends. Caroline's big ambition in life is to be beautiful. With the help of a lot of make-up, she just about is. She's also as two-faced as you can get — a born user.

For example, she wants me to go out and

celebrate my birthday. Not for my sake, of course. What she has in mind is to pretend we're going to the Trax, an underage club, but actually hit Glades nightclub outside town, where she can down a few bottles of Bud and smoke her brains out.

Anyway, like I said, Mam has other ideas. We're going to a new restaurant in town.

'Just the two of us,' she announces. 'It'll be nice. We can talk.'

I'm getting out of the car and she adds, 'We need to talk,' but I'm not listening. I'm watching the moving forest of green uniforms. If I go in among them, I'll be lost, invisible again with my long hair and patient silence. And nothing to look forward to but dinner in a fancy restaurant.

The car pulls away and I go back home.

*

In the morning quiet of the house, I sit on the hallway floor, waiting for my father's cheque to drop in through the letterbox. The bang of the flap disturbs my calm only a little.

At the bank, I cash the cheque first. Then I ask for Mam. There are tears in her eyes when I tell her what I want to do, but she doesn't make too much of a fuss.

At the door, I turn back to see if she's okay. She's on the phone, and I wonder if she could possibly be talking to my father.

I don't have an appointment at the hairdressers, so there's a wait. School's out for lunch when I get back. The lunch hall is packed, but it's curiously silent as I walk up to Caroline's table. The thick make-up is no mask for her surprise.

'What time are we going out?' I ask.

*

Glades nightclub is a big cement box, full of flashing lights. Caroline has plastered so much mascara on my face, I don't know who I'm looking at in the ladies-room mirror. I'm in no hurry to go back out. Caroline has met up with a bunch of bimbos and they've spent the last hour discussing Cher — her face-lifts, her toy-boys. They keep asking me what I think of an older woman going out with a twenty-five-year-old. As if I care. I'm hoping they'll have moved on to something else when I get back.

They have. 'He's coming this way!' one of Caroline's friends squeals. 'I told you he always fancied you. You'll have to dance with him.'

'No way.' Caroline is on her feet, stubbing out her cigarette and moving away.

'But you used to fancy him too,' another bimbo says, 'before …'

'Yeah,' Caroline answers, her lipsticked mouth wrinkled in disgust. 'Before.'

She's gone and the others have legged it after her. Glad to be left alone, I sit down. My wishbone box almost slips out of my combats pocket as I fish out the change to ring for a taxi home.

Standing above me are two guys. One of them

whispers something in his friend's ear and limps away, smirking. The other is a regular poser. Black hair, gelled into spikes; the glint of a ring in his left eyebrow, which I can just make out above his dark shades. I'm turning away when I notice this odd, panicked look on his face that makes me nervous. His lost, dumb stare starts getting to me.

'What are you gawking at?'

'Will you dance?' he asks. 'Please.'

I'm not nervous now. I'm afraid. His 'please' is childlike. I shake my head. *Before?* Caroline fancied him *before* what?

'Will you dance? Please,' he repeats.

'I was just going.' I'm worried he won't let me pass. I try squeezing by him. The gelled hair can't hide the raw groove of scar running from his temple to the back of his head. Something's happened to slow down his brain, I'm thinking, make a child of him.

'Okay, then,' I tell him, but he doesn't move.

'You'll have to take my hand.'

'Sorry?'

There's the lovely flash of a shy, uncertain smile before his sallow features darken over again. 'I'm blind.'

*

Half past twelve, and the Supersnax is quiet before the late-night rush. The smell of meat grease rots the air. The Coke I'm sipping is flat and treacly. His story is sour with despair and sugared with self-pity. I'm flattered when he tells me I'm the first one he's ever really opened up to; and uneasy, too. Gary McCann is a dark cloud waiting to burst, and he's no innocent.

Six months ago he and his friend Shay stole a car from outside the New Cinema and went joyriding. On the straight stretch of the Racecourse Road, the front left tyre blew out. The car hit the ditch and sailed over. Gary went through the windscreen. His friend was thrown out the passenger door and broke his femur.

He feels like he's lost everything — football, films, his computer graphics, late-night hanging out, everything he lived for. I have no idea what to say. All I can do is listen.

Sometimes the listening's easy. Things he's saying ring so many bells that my head feels like a church steeple. His parents treating him like a charity case, a half-step behind him all hours of the day. Fussing about him going to Glades tonight — his first night out since the crash. Planning a life for him — 'All the things you can still do, Gary' — that he doesn't want. Showering him with gifts he doesn't care for.

'I suppose it can't be easy for them,' I say, surprising myself, and his jaw tightens. There's a throbbing above his ear where the scar starts. The crowd from Glades is beginning to drift in, and I'm getting uncomfortable. It seems selfish, but I wish I could see some more of that flashing smile and the lightness he had when we danced ('Celine Dion! Drowning's too good for her'). Gary's retreated into his darkness. Then he draws me right in there with him.

'The terrible thing is,' he says, 'I can still see when I dream. Sometimes I'm afraid to sleep.'

I put my hand on his. Just as I do, a gang of messers makes a noisy entrance. Gary's friend, the one with the limp, is among them. I get a bad feeling as they gather, sniggering, at a table near us. Then Caroline takes one step inside the door, looks at me like I have two heads, one weirder than the other, and shoots back out.

'I've dreamt about you,' Gary says. 'At least I got to see you before …'

My hand leaves his, of its own accord. The crash was six months ago, I'm thinking.

'I'm only in town two months,' I say, as much to myself as to him.

'I thought … Shay said … You're Caroline Hanley, right?'

There's a loud guffaw from Shay, and his pals join in. I suppose it's my blushing face that sets them off. I leave my seat and head for the door. Gary is muttering threateningly. It feels like everyone in Supersnax is laughing at me.

My reflection in the glass door is a stranger telling me I can't leave — not without a fight.

They duck their heads as one when I make for their table. Suddenly the place is like a morgue. My fingers grip the wishbone box for courage.

'Lucky Gary, to have a friend like you,' I say. 'This is your idea of a joke, is it?'

Shay looks up. His grin is all off-kilter; it looks like a twist of pain.

'Yeah,' he answers. 'And Gary's idea of a joke is

bringing me for a ride and leaving me crippled.'

'He forced you into the car, did he?'

'Get lost — *Caroline*.'

The laughing starts up again, but the roar from Gary cuts it off. Shay is jumping out of his seat as I spin around and see Gary charging blindly towards us.

'I'll have you, Shay!' he's screaming.

Shay pushes past me so roughly that my thigh slams into the corner of the table. I feel the box breaking in my pocket. They're in the centre aisle and Shay is the cocky bullfighter to Gary's pain-blinded bull. I take the pieces from my pocket. Crushed velvet and splinters of bone fill my palm. Gary crashes into table after table, knocking over beakers of Coke and cartons of chips.

'You broke my wishbone!' I feel stupid because I'm getting odd looks and because I'm still dumb enough to believe in the magic of bones.

The floor is a sticky mess. My stomach sickens at their manic laughter when Gary slips, slams into another table and goes down hard. I strike out and land a perfect five-fingered stinger on Shay's cheek.

It's like a full stop. Shay looks like he's woken from a bad dream. Gary is halfway under a table, covering his eyes.

'Where are my shades?' he pleads, but they're smashed to bits around the floor.

I want to help him, to pick him up and lead him home. But I don't think he wants to be helped — or maybe I'm just making excuses for myself, for feeling too hurt to help him. I think he wants to find his own way through the dark. I find myself wishing he can.

I carve a path through the silence and out the door.

*

Did I say 'full stop'? Here's me thinking my big day of rebellion is ending in tears over an old bone. Seeing nothing, running, turning the corner into our street. Me at the low timber gate — stopping dead. There's a flash red car I've never seen before in the drive, the kind my father might go for.

I'm halfway up the tarmac drive when the front door opens and there's Mam, holding hands with a fair-haired stranger. He seems very young. All Caroline's bitchy talk about Cher clicks into place.

I suppose Mam expects me to slag her off for keeping this secret from me, and to fire some abuse in Paul's direction too. And it's there, on the tip of my tongue, ready to be said, to be spat out. But I think of Gary, flailing wildly back at Supersnax and hurting no one but himself.

I ask, 'Aren't you going to introduce me?'

'I didn't plan this,' Mam says. 'I was upset. Paul came over to —'

'Mam,' I say. 'You don't have to explain. Just stop treating me like I don't exist, like I don't have a brain, like I'm a child. Okay?'

I turn to her friend, who's trying to find

somewhere to put his hands. I offer him mine.
'Hello, Paul.'

*

In my room, I wait for Mam to climb the stairs. She doesn't come to look in on me; instead, she calls 'Good night,' from the landing. It leaves me lonely. I hold my shattered lucky charm as if the tightness of my grip might meld the pieces together again.

One o'clock. Quarter past. Half past. I don't sleep. I keep remembering what Gary said about being afraid to dream. There are things I don't want to dream about, too. Chicken dinners, and fairytale reunions — and Gary, I suppose. I'm uneasy, too, about being so hard on Mam all day. It seems like — as usual — my dad has got the easy side of the bargain.

An idea grows in me. At a quarter to two, I sneak down to the hallway. I take the phone into the dining-room and leave a message on his answering machine. As I speak, I toss the remnants of box and bone into the empty mouth of the fireplace.

'It's me. I don't think I want to go to Budapest. I'm kind of busy next month,' I say, after the beep. 'And, by the way, I've got my hair cut. Talk to you again, Dad.'

I can't think of any more to say, but I still haven't put the phone down. I'm sure that when Dad hears the message, he'll be wondering what the racket at the end is all about, because I'm wondering too. Then I realise it's someone banging on the front door.

Mam is at the top of the stairs when I nervously inch back the door.

The dark shades are gone. I see the whites beneath the scarred, half-closed eyelids. His black hair has collapsed into a sticky mess. His denim jacket is torn along the sleeve and there's blood trickling from his arm.

'Gary!' I exclaim. 'Did Shay do this to you?'

'Nah, I wrecked myself in Supersnax.'

'Who brought you here?'

'No one,' he says, with a touch of wry pride. 'I made it here myself.'

'But how did you find me?' I ask, as if anything matters except that he searched the night for me. 'You don't even know my name.'

'I asked. Eva Looney, right?' he says, like he can't bear to be wrong again. 'I had to see you.'

Suddenly he seems to realise what he's just said, and he starts to laugh, and I do too. It's like we're stepping into the light together, into some brighter, more un-self-pitying place than either of us could have wished for.

Mam insists that he come in, and she makes coffee for us and patches his arm up. Then she leaves us alone for a little while. It doesn't feel like she's hovering. It just feels like she's there, which is okay.

There's an odd moment when Gary asks me to describe myself to him. What can I say? Short red hair — *very* short red hair. Brown eyes with green flecks. Freckles — too many of them — along my nose and under my eyes. Not tall, not small. It's all very vague, but it's enough for Gary to make a picture of me in his mind, he says.

'What's this stuff about the wishbone?' he wants to know. 'You freaked out over that.'

'*I* freaked out?' I say lightly; but I'm touched that he noticed my distress as he raged through his own.

So I tell him about a long-ago chicken dinner. And I'm thinking that maybe there's nothing worth wishing for but moments like this, when there's nothing you need to wish for.

Millennia

CORA HARRISON

It was Drumshee; but it was not Drumshee as she knew it. The modern building, with its computers and its fax machine, had vanished, and so had the four-hundred-year-old cottage.

The fort was there, but it wasn't the same, somehow. The surrounding ditch was wider, deeper; the stone walls on top of the bank were taller. The gateway looked almost menacing.

She paused at the foot of the hill. It was growing dark. The constellation of Orion had risen in the south-western sky above the fort. She should be getting inside the enclosure. She looked around fearfully.

Then she heard it — faint at first, then louder, still in the distance but coming nearer at a fast running pace. She knew the sound, and her blood curdled within her. The wolves were coming!

She could hear the thudding of their feet as they came down the hill. Soon they would be on top of her. She could never hope to outrun them. She had no time to reach the safety of the fort and its enclosing walls.

Quickly she turned back. If she could get to the river before they crossed, her scent might be lost. She plunged over the uneven ground, trying to avoid the ensnaring arms of the briars. The vicious thorns tore at her leg, and blood ran down into her sandal and onto the ground beneath her. It didn't matter. Its smell would only serve to lead the wolves up the hill and away from the river. She ran on.

In another minute she was in the water. She moved quietly into the centre of the river and began to swim downstream.

She heard the wolves cross the River Fergus, and then a great howl rose up from the leader. He had smelt her blood. This would delay them; but they would be back. They would return to the river.

She swam on steadily; but a few minutes later she realised, with a great gulp of panic, that the wolves had returned. She heard the first of them entering the water, and then the splashes as the others followed. Hastily she dipped her head beneath the water and stayed down for as long as her bursting lungs would allow.

When she lifted her head for a moment, she thought they had gone. She could hear nothing — nothing except the drumming of her blood in her eardrums. She kept swimming, though, and as the water cleared from her ears she heard them again. They weren't sure, though. Some seemed to be going upstream, and some, she knew, were still on the bank where she had cut her leg. Again the eerie howl rose up, and again the other wolves responded with a series of short barks and excited yelps.

She could swim no further. In this limestone land, the river went underground at this spot. She could see the place where it plunged down: a dark, steep cavern, its sides streaming with water. To go down it would mean near-certain death, she guessed. The rocks were sharp and jagged-edged, and she would be certain to lose her footing on the loose, sliding scree between them. She could hear the thunder of the water crashing down on the rocks below.

She wavered, looked back over her shoulder, and then made up her mind. The wolves weren't sure yet; but they were moving downstream towards her, tumbling in and out of the water, running back to sniff the briars and then coming on again. For the moment, the water had confused the scent; but soon they would find her.

Taking a deep breath, she plunged under the water again and let the force of it carry her over the edge of the cavern. She didn't know whether she would be dashed to pieces by the protruding rocks as she fell; she didn't even know whether there was any depth of water at the bottom, or whether she would crash down among sharp rocks. All she knew was that anything would be better than being torn apart by a pack of wolves.

Desperately she clawed at a piece of rock, trying to break the force and the speed of her fall. The sharp edge of its broken surface tore the skin of her hand and, without meaning to, she cried out. The cry was immediately answered by a howl from the wolves. They knew where she was now. They had heard the cry and they could smell the fresh blood. They filled the mouth of the cavern in their eagerness to get at her, their ravenous desire to taste the blood they smelt.

Then, miraculously, she was on her feet, up to her knees in water, her arms securely locked around a stout pillar of rock — safe for the moment. There was no hope of swimming, though; swimming would be quickest, but the water was far too shallow. She stumbled down the rocky bed of the river, the swirling water almost knocking her down.

Quickly she risked a glance over her shoulder. The wolves hadn't trusted to the water to carry them down, but were slipping and sliding down the wet, moss-covered rocks. If only she could keep ahead of them ... She knew where the river came above ground again, and she knew that if she could get there, she might be safe.

The wolves had reached the bottom and were racing along the river. Their howls filled the cavern and echoed around and around, making her feel sick and dizzy. With all her strength she pulled a stone from a ledge and threw it amongst them. A chorus of yelps rose. Her aim had been sure. It would not delay them long, but she could hear them snapping and growling at one another.

This might gain her the vital few minutes.

Above her head was daylight. A swallow hole, no water flooding down it at the moment, but still too steep for her to climb. But no, that wouldn't be the way ... Yes, there it was, just ahead of her: a left-hand turn.

She stopped and threw another stone. That was her second one; she wouldn't get another chance. It worked, though. Once again, a scuffle broke out amongst the wolves.

Then she was out in the open, desperately running.

In front of her was a lake. There had been a settlement on it once — a *crannóg*, it was called; she remembered hearing about that. The settlement had been built up on piles of logs and brushwood in the very centre of the lake. There was no one living there any more, but the bridge across the lake still stood. It was made from thin planks of wood, strung on great ropes of rawhide, and it swung and tilted as she put her feet on it. She didn't hesitate, however. This was the way. She was sure of that.

Behind her, the wolves poured out of the underground cavern. They saw her, and a great howl of triumph rose up. The leader ran to the bridge; but when his feet touched the swaying planks, he hesitated and drew back. Others tried to push past him, but they, too, drew back as soon as their feet touched the unsteady surface. They howled their frustration and anger to the skies. Several of them ran up and down the shore of the lake.

She reached the settlement. There was no one there. She had expected that. There were still some traces of the wooden houses left, though. One of them must hold something which would be of use to her. Frantically she searched through hut after hut.

And one hut had something in it. She didn't see it at first; then a stray gleam of sunshine picked up a flash of gold from a dark corner. She ran over.

It was a gold ring. It was too big for her finger, but it fitted snugly around her thumb. She stared down at it. On it were two words in the ancient Ogham script, cut into the soft gold with a knife.

She had known she might find something like this, and she was prepared. Hesitantly she spelt out the message.

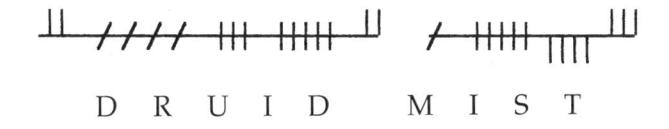

D R U I D   M I S T

Puzzled, she scrutinised it for a moment, willing herself to understand, but it meant nothing to her.

She ran out of the hut and looked across the lake. The wolves had begun to swim across, their heads breaking the surface as they cut smoothly through the water. She gave them one panic-stricken glance and then ran into the last hut.

And there was something that might be useful

— a bronze axe. She snatched it up and went back to the edge of the water, near the swinging bridge.

Her heart was thudding, but she forced herself to wait calmly until the moment when the wolves reached the shore and came running past the deserted huts, straight towards her. Holding her axe firmly, she launched herself onto the bridge, going as fast as she could, keeping one hand on the rawhide rope.

Once again, the wolves tried to follow her onto the bridge; but once again they hesitated. The leader fell back; the younger members of the pack jostled for his place and then fell back in turn. The scuffling and bad temper broke out again, but she didn't turn to look. She went on, as swiftly as she could. She knew what would happen next.

This time the wolves were even quicker in their decision. By the time she had reached the far shore, the leaders had already taken to the water. She had only a few moments before her life was in danger again.

This time she didn't turn back towards the river. She knew that they could go faster than she on that rocky riverbed. She looked around desperately. On the side of the hill above her was a huge, ancient tomb, a court tomb, with a faint webbing of mist drifting above it. It was the mist that caught her attention first, but then she looked at the tomb. Was there a chance that she could hide there — could escape, perhaps? There might be another way out. These ancient tombs were always riddled with passageways, she knew that. Holding the bronze axe firmly in her hand, she raced up the hill.

The entrance was right in front of her, facing east, of course. It looked securely shut, but when she pressed the portal stone, the rock slid back. She wasted precious moments trying to close it behind her. Then she heard the drumming of the wolves' feet on the hillside. She abandoned her efforts and fled down the passageway.

Then all was silent — and she felt all the more frightened because of that silence.

At the end of the passageway was a small circular room, and lying on the ground were several skeletons. One of them had been a druid, she guessed; the dry air of the tomb had preserved the remains of his flowing robe, and clutched in the long white bones of his hand was a piece of mistletoe, its berries brown and shrivelled. She didn't stop to look at him. She was desperately searching for a way out.

The wolves were right behind her. With a howl of triumph they burst into the room, scattering the ancient bones on the floor.

She gave one hunted glance around and then flung the bronze axe at the wall above her, just below a high stone ledge. The sharp metal head stuck in a crevice between two stones, and she grasped the handle and swung herself up to crouch on the narrow ledge. The wolves rose up on their hind legs and snapped and growled within inches of her, but they could reach no higher.

There was a gap in the rock behind her. Could she go through it? Using all her strength, she pushed a loose rock away from the gap and squeezed through. She delayed a moment longer, to push the stone back into place; it might block the wolves for a few extra minutes, if they did succeed in scrambling up the wall of the tomb.

That had been the right move. Suddenly she was out in the open. She stood for a moment, looking around. There was a grove of oak trees at the top of the hill; if she could reach them, she might be able to climb a tree and spend the night there, safe from the wolves. Rapidly she moved up the hill, the howling of the wolves inside the tomb still following her. Faster, she thought. I must get there before they get free.

She entered the blackness of the oak grove. She put a hand on the rough bark of a tree, still slightly uncertain of her next move.

It was a mistake. She knew that a moment later. Suddenly the air was filled with the raucous cawing of a million black ravens. They rose up from the trees where they had been roosting and crowded around her, their sharp beaks jabbing at her eyes, their wings beating against her head.

She fumbled at her belt for the bronze axe, then remembered that she had left it in the tomb. If only she had a weapon! An iron knife, perhaps? That might be it ... Shielding her head with her arms, she searched desperately around the tree-trunks. There must be *something* ...

By the time she found the weapon, slung on

the low branch of a lightning-blasted oak, her cheeks and arms were bleeding, but her eyes were safe. The weapon wasn't an iron knife, though; it was a golden sickle, its curved knife-edge gleaming in the light of the rising moon. She picked it up and waved it around her head. The moon shining on the blade made a circle of golden light between her and the ravens. Around and around she whirled, keeping the sickle moving, keeping the birds of doom away from her. They screamed their rage, and their cries had a weird human-like note.

And their shrieks were echoed by the deeper, more menacing sound from the tomb. It was getting louder, the noise of the wolves. She knew what that meant: they had come close to the way out. Soon they would join the ravens.

Think, she said to herself. There must be a way out. There always is. Once again she waved the golden sickle, and once again its magical powers drove the ravens back.

That was it! Suddenly she understood. She remembered the druid skeleton in the tomb, with the mistletoe clasped in its fleshless hand. The golden sickle was used by the ancient druids to cut mistletoe. Her eyes stabbed the gathering darkness, scanning the trunks of the oak trees. There must be mistletoe somewhere. If she could find it and cut it off with the golden sickle, she could invoke the powers of the druids to help her escape.

And there it was — the cluster of marble-white berries, gleaming against the rough bark of an oak tree on the other side of the grove. It wasn't too high up; she could easily reach it. With renewed courage she spun around, slashing at the ravens, driving them back, giving herself the space to cross the open centre of the oak grove.

Three quick steps and she was across. The ravens drew back, frightened now by more than the menace of the golden sickle. She must be within the mistletoe's magic circle of power, perhaps even within the magic powers of the sacred druids themselves. Whatever it was, she didn't hesitate. She grasped the mistletoe with her left hand and quickly slashed it free from the trunk with her sickle.

It was not a moment too soon. With something halfway between a howl and a scream, the first of the wolves burst out of the tomb. With a chorus of yelps and barks and growls, the rest followed. Their feet drummed like thunder as they raced up the hill towards their prey.

She stood firm. She had made all the right moves; she believed that. Now all she had to do was invoke the magic power of the druids. Her mind searched urgently for the right words.

Then she remembered the ring she had found in the deserted house on the *crannóg*. Quickly she glanced down at it. This time the letters were quite clear. 'Druid mist,' they spelled. That was what the druids were able to bestow on their followers: the magical mist that hid them from their enemies.

Hastily she laid the golden sickle on the ground. She drew the ring off her thumb and threw it straight in the face of the leading wolf.

Almost instantly, she found that everything had gone a strange grey-white. There was no sound — no sound from the ravens, no sound from the wolves. For a moment she wondered if something terrible had happened.

And then, in a flash, she understood. The spell had worked. She was alone inside the protection of the druidic mist.

Still holding the mistletoe and the golden sickle, she moved forward confidently. She couldn't see her way, but she believed that nothing could go wrong now. The mist wouldn't last long, she knew that; and as long as she didn't go in the wrong direction, she would be safe.

Her eyes strained to see through the swirl of grey and white. And there it was: she could just make out the constellation of Orion, high in the sky before her. She moved towards it happily. She knew she had done the right thing.

The mist cleared, and she was outside the gates of Drumshee.

With a click of the mouse button she was through, and the gates of the Drumshee fort closed safely behind her.

Emma sat back in her chair and sighed happily. She had done it!

'It's brilliant, Dad,' she said, watching the multicoloured 'The End' graphic appear across the fort on her screen. 'It's the best one in your whole *Millennia* series.'

FROM THE BIG ISLAND

Sabotage

DAVID CADDY

I had to get to the supermarket!

I had never ridden faster. Some people wouldn't even have seen me. They'd feel a rush of wind, and they'd turn around, but I'd be gone, just a blur.

The front wheel was wobbling. I had to keep it in control. If I came off at this speed, there'd be a horrible mess over the road. I'd be splattered for miles. But, I had my helmet on. I could go faster. I pushed into my pedals and accelerated.

Down the hill. Up the hill. Heading towards a set of traffic lights. The lights were green. I was thirty metres away. The lights went orange. I was ten metres away. I was going too fast to stop, so I pedaled faster. A car was turning in front of me. It slammed to a halt, and I heard abuse. I was through the red light, going downhill. 'Yeeha!' I screamed to the sky.

The sky laughed back, or maybe it was a kookaburra!

Racing down hill.

There was Smithson's Supermarket! Gleaming in the sunlight, white and red and golden. What a supermarket! This was the ideal place for my first job.

Just as long as I could lie about my age! I wasn't very good at lying, and I blame my mother for that. 'When you lie it gets bigger and bigger until it's as plain as the nose on your face.'

But I had to lie! My friend Sean did, when he got a job. He's been working there for three months. 'Don't worry about it. Who's going to check up on you? You're only a kid!' he said.

I slowed down. There was a speed bump. If I hit it this fast I'd end up through the automatic doors and into the freezer department before I could stop. I didn't have air brakes.

I leaned into my handbrakes. The wheels squealed! Screamed! I could imagine the sparks flying out. I hoped there were no dead leaves around. The last thing I wanted on my first day at work was a bush fire!

Finally, my bike was slow enough. I leaped off, padlocked my front wheel, and ran to the automatic doors. Thud! The automatic doors don't open fast enough. A checkout girl had seen me. I hope she's not on the interviewing panel.

I raced in. Thwonk! The metal bars that spin around to let you into the store don't spin fast enough. My thigh was hurting.

I slowed down and jogged past the women's

underwear, and straight to the office window.

Oh no! There stood Anna Brody. 'What are you doing here?' I asked, narrowing my eyes. I knew full well what she was doing here. She was after my job.

'I'm applying for the job.'

'It's mine,' I answered, trying to sound tougher than I was. 'Sean told me about it. You must have overheard him.'

'What if I did?'

'It's my job,' I growled.

'Who says so?' A voice from the office asked.

I gulped. I blushed.

'You don't even look old enough!'

'I am,' I lied. 'I'm the same age as Anna, here.' That was the truth.

There was a long silence. The voice in the office was thinking.

'I'll put you both on, Anna for the first week and you for the second. Whoever has the smoothest week gets the job. Fair enough!'

'Fair enough,' blurted Anna.

'But it's supposed to be my job!' I pleaded.

'Look kid. She was here first. All you've done is complain. Take the second week, or I'll give the job to her. What's your choice?'

'Sure!' I replied, trying to sound positive, enthusiastic, agreeable — all those things that Sean had said I should be.

My bike was leaden. The wheels turned slowly. Anna was starting on Monday. A week later I was going to have my turn. What chance did I have?

Anna was a straight A student. She had gorgeous brown eyes, long chestnut hair and just the greatest tan. Even in winter she had a tan.

She was a quick learner and good at whatever she did. In our class she was tops at everything!

'Where's my ice-cream?' It was Sean.

'What?'

'You said you'd buy me an ice-cream when you got the job.'

'Anna Brody and I turned up at the same time. We've both got a trial of one week. Whoever has the smoothest week gets the job!'

'Anna Brody?'

'Yep!'

'What's your problem? Make sure she doesn't have the smoothest week!'

'What do you mean?'

'Sabotage!'

Sabotage meant disguise but the only thing in the house with a hood was my sister's raincoat. I tried my mum's stockings, but they have diamond love hearts down the back and frilly black lace. They look ridiculous and you have trouble seeing through them. I'd just have to keep a low profile.

On Monday after school, Sean and I rode to Smithson's. I made it through the automatic doors without smashing my face. Then I walked through the spinning bar without bruising my thighs. Sean went and talked with a checkout girl.

I was in the store, and I was on my own.

I saw Anna Brody at checkout number one. I sneaked through 'Women's Underwear' and into 'Houseware'. There it was, a whole shelf of mouse and rat traps. There were hundreds of them. I took one out and looked around. No one was there. My breathing was heavy. I leaned over the shelf and carefully set the traps.

'Hey you!' a deep voice called over my shoulder.

I jumped. It was Sean, laughing. 'Mongrel,' I sighed. 'Help me.'

'No mate! I'm happy to distract others and keep lookout, but I don't want to lose my job. I'll go talk to Anna.'

For ten minutes I carefully loaded the traps. A few people walked past, but I acted pretty cool. When I had finished I was shaking uncontrollably. It was thrilling.

The next aisle was 'Tinned Goods'. There was one great stack of baked beans, reaching almost to the ceiling. There must have been about two thousand cans of baked beans. Enough gas there to run a heater for a month. Sean was still with Anna. I moved one of the bottom tins right to the edge so that it was only just supporting the tins above it. The slightest bump, shake, or wind would cause the whole lot to come tumbling down.

The sabotage was almost finished. There was one more thing to do.

I bought a block of chocolate and, as Sean and I went through the checkout, I left one mousetrap on the counter.

Loitering at the entrance we heard a call over the intercom. 'Miss Brody! Front end! Please.' We saw her pick up the mousetrap. We saw her walk between the aisles. She was returning the one mousetrap to where it belonged. I would probably have just chucked it in there, but not Anna. She would place it neatly into its correct shelf.

We heard a scream, and someone went running from the checkouts. I wonder how many mousetraps had gotten her!

I went home and spent an hour in the woodpile collecting bugs.

Tuesday afternoon I walked, fairly confidently, into Smithson's.

The baked beans hadn't collapsed. Why hadn't anyone bumped them? Why hadn't they fallen over in the night? There were a zillion cans there. Oh well, there were other things to do.

Sean was talking to Anna. What a star! I crept into 'Houseware'. I wound up every clock in the rack, set every alarm in the store and I had done it beautifully. I crept back to 'Women's Underwear' and waited.

'RRRIIIINNNNNNGGGGG! Ring! Cuckoo! Cuckoo!'

'Miss Brody! Front end please!'

We saw Anna being talked to. She rushed off to the clocks. She turned off one, and then another, and another.

Just as she arrived back at her checkout job, the alarms rang out again.

'Miss Brody! Front end please!'

Anna was talked to a bit more severely this time. She ran to 'Houseware' and turned off the alarms. She also hit every other alarm switch to turn them all off. What she didn't see were the twenty alarm clocks that had somehow moved to another aisle. Ten minutes later, they went off.

'Miss Brody!' came a rather harsh voice over the intercom.

'You really got her then,' said Sean.

'Yep!'

'She was even told off.'

'Yep! It was cool to watch heh?'

Sean didn't say anything.

A nice block of chocolate and a leisurely ride home was a wonderful reward. Before the day ended I spent another hour in the woodpile.

I plotted all of Wednesday. It was excellent.

What was the one thing Anna was called to do? Check prices!

I couldn't go around changing all the prices, it would take too long. But there was something I could do!

I sneaked through 'Women's Underwear' and into the food aisles.

At ten different places in each aisle there were 'Specials' signs, with reduced prices. I quickly collected the signs and put them out again. It was risky work, and it was slow work, but it was easy, and with good rewards. One hundred 'Special' signs were on the wrong articles. I didn't see Sean at all — he'd spent the whole time talking to Anna.

As we left the store there was a woman having a fierce argument with the checkout supervisor.

'Miss Brody! Price check! Counter 4!'

'Miss Brody! Price check! Counter 7!'

'Miss Brody!'

Sean said that maybe I'd gone a bit over the top, and I should cool it.

At school on Thursday I almost mucked up. I asked Anna how it was going. She looked at me suspiciously and asked me why I was asking her. I blushed, made up an excuse and exited quickly.

Thursday afternoon I was getting desperate.

First stop was the cleaning aisle. I unscrewed the tops of all the containers of detergents and washing-up liquids. Second stop was a food aisle. I rotated the stock, so the stale food was in the fresh food section at the front, and the quick use-by date food was at the back. My last stop was 'Biscuits and Beverages'. I set the coffee grinder going with no cup under it, grabbed a block of chocolate and went through the checkout. Sean seemed angry. He said that enough was enough, and he wouldn't join me for chocolate.

I spent the afternoon searching in the garden, eating my block of chocolate and scheming.

On Friday, after school, I rode home before going to Smithson's. This was my last chance to make Anna's week hellish. I picked up my lunch box, full of cockroaches from the woodpile and wood louse from around the garden. I had millions of them.

At Smithson's I ran as many trolleys as I could

find to the far end of the carpark and as I entered the store, I switched off the automatic doors. Then I went straight to 'Fruit and Vegetables' and unleashed the bugs, scattering cockroaches as I went. I saw someone tip over a bottle of detergent. I heard someone complaining at the front counter about the use-by date. There were people queuing up, trying to get into the store, but the door wouldn't open. Some were getting angry.

And I saw Anna running left and right. She even ran down the tinned food section and knocked the stack of baked beans. Hundreds of cans fell and clattered and clanked. Then I saw Sean going to help her. I smiled at him but he glared back.

The shop was in chaos — no way in the world was Anna going to get that job!

That evening I phoned Sean to thank him for his help but he wasn't home. His mum said he'd gone out to the pictures with Anna Brody. I struggled to talk but couldn't. Anna Brody and Sean! I tried not to think about it.

On Sunday morning I was so excited about my new job. I dug into my cupboard and found my long black trousers and white shirt. Mum showed me how to operate the washing machine, and afterwards I hung the clothes on the line. I polished my shoes and left them on the verandah, out the front. I practised my smile in front of the mirror and bought an extra block of chocolate from the corner store for Sean.

That afternoon I went to bring my clothes in

but they were off the line, in the dirt! How did that happen? I'd have to wash them again.

Monday afternoon, I raced home from school to get ready but I couldn't find my shoes anywhere. I knew I'd left them on the verandah. Where were they? I eventually found them in the garden, filled with soil! I brushed them out as best I could but I was running out of time. My clothes were still damp too. I'd have to live with that.

I ran to the bike but the tyres were flat and the pump was missing. Talk about bad luck. Where was the pump? There, in the garden. I'd have to rush. Ninety-three pumps later and the tyres were up. I leaped onto the seat and pedaled out the gate. I had to move fast now, but what was this, something yucky on my seat. It was chocolate! How had chocolate gotten on my bike seat?

I couldn't turn back. I was going to be late as it was. Through the gate and up the hill I cycled. I'd have to be careful how I walked around the store. I'd have to hold my hands behind my back.

Finally I arrived but I was ten minutes late. I plonked my bike down, and hurried to the office. I heard Sean inside, he must have been waiting for me.

Then I heard Anna's voice! 'There he is, re-organising all the special signs and there he is, stacking the baked beans.'

'He's swapping the fresh food around,' said Sean.

I peeked around the corner. The manager was

with them. 'And setting the mouse traps and releasing cockroaches in my store! Wait till he gets here.'

The three of them were huddled over a security monitor. I swallowed heavily and edged back from the door.

I heard Sean again. 'How do the cameras work?' he asked.

'You just press this button and select the camera,' the manager answered. 'See!'

'There he is right now,' shouted Anna.

I looked up. A camera! I ran! Through 'Women's Underwear'. Over the metal bar! Out the automatic door. Thud! It still doesn't open fast enough. I leaped onto my bike. I had never ridden faster. Some people wouldn't even have seen me. They'd feel a rush of wind, and they'd turn around, but I'd be gone, just a blur.

Popocatapetl

DEBORAH LISSON

Some kids collect stamps or autographs, I collect words. One of them is bomb. Bomb is a beautiful word to say, but it's an even better one to look at. You have to write it big, like this, **b o m b**, round and heavy and solid. You can imagine the O with a lighted fuse sticking out of it, like a bomb in a cartoon drawing.

Another of my favourites is lamentation, but that's a word you have to say aloud. It drops out of your mouth like rain and reminds me of angels and waterfalls and the plinking of a music box.

Sometimes I collect whole sentences. A couple of months ago Dad came in after drenching the sheep and said 'If we don't get some rain soon we'll have to sell off more of last year's lambs.' I collected the last bit of that. 'Last year's lambs,' it has such a forlorn and lonely sound. When I want to make myself sad I stand on the hill overlooking our farm and say it to myself, out loud, very slowly.

By now you're probably thinking I'm a real dork. That's why I've never told anyone about my word collection, not Mum and Dad, or any of the kids at school, and specially I've never told Mr Brennan.

Mr Brennan is our class teacher. He despairs of me. I know because he tells me so — often. 'Sarah, Sarah,' he says when I forget my homework or don't get my class assignments finished on time, 'whatever am I going to do with you?' and he shakes his head sadly and all the class laughs.

Mr Brennan has favourite words too, but I don't think he knows it. One of them is 'concentrate'. 'Concentrate, Sarah,' he tells me, 'pay attention and concentrate. Nobody ever won a Brownlow Medal by daydreaming.' He talks a lot about Brownlow Medals. That's because he used to be a footballer, but his knees packed up on him, so he had to train as a teacher instead. Sometimes I think he'd rather be playing football.

Today when we came into class, he said he had something to tell us. 'We have an author visiting the school,' he announced. 'Her name is Angela Mason and after lunch she will be coming to this class to talk to you about writing.'

I was thrilled. I've always wanted to meet a real live author, but no one else seemed very excited.

'Does that mean we'll have to miss sport, sir?'

asked Jason Higgins.

'Yes, I'm afraid it does.'

The boys groaned.

'Is she famous?' asked Janina Prentice.

'I don't know, said Mr Brennan. 'I don't read a lot of children's books.'

'Why do we have to have a writer,' whinged Jason. 'Why can't we have a footballer or a famous cricketer instead.'

'Because we can't always have what we want,' said Mr Brennan. I could tell he was trying not to laugh. 'I'm sure Mrs Mason will have some very interesting things to tell us, and I expect you all to be on your best behaviour.'

After that he gave us back the stories we had done for homework, and straight away I was in trouble again. Actually, they weren't really stories. They were letters. Mr Brennan thinks we should care about what is happening in our community, so he made us write pretend letters to the local council about the mall they want to make in Victoria Street. He said as community opinion was divided on the subject our letters should reflect this. That meant some of us had to be for the mall and some had to be against it.

I was picked to be against, though really I'd much rather have been for the mall. I think it's a neat idea. For ages I couldn't think of anything to write. Then I started picturing Victoria Street with all the traffic gone and the paving down and in my mind I could see the pattern made by the paving stones. It reminded me of a poem I read when I was little. It was about a small boy walking in a London street, and it said when you walk on a pavement you must never tread on the lines, because if you do, bears will get you.

I sat for a long time thinking about that, imagining the bears and thinking how careful you would have to be, and how you would never be able to daydream when you were out shopping. It gave me a great idea and I made my letter to the council a warning about what might happen if they turned Victoria Street into a mall. I asked them if they really wanted bears lurking round every corner, and what the shopkeepers would say if all their customers got eaten. And then I said what about babies in prams, how could you wheel a pram on a pavement without going over the lines?

The more I wrote, the more new things I thought of. It turned into quite a long letter and I thought it was pretty good. But when I saw it still sitting on Mr Brennan's desk after he'd given all the others back I knew he didn't agree with me. He called me up to the front and read some of it to the class. Then he shook his head and did his 'Sarah, Sarah,' thing. After that he said, 'I wanted an intelligent argument, Sarah, not fairy floss. A well written letter is supposed to inform people, not waft them off into lala land.'

Everyone thought that was very funny,

From then on the day just got worse. We did maths after recess. I really did try to concentrate and for half a page everything went fine. But then I noticed something interesting. There was a pattern in some of the numbers I'd written — a row of eights going down the page, one exactly under the other. If you linked them up, they'd look a bit like a paper chain and that set me thinking about this story I've started writing in my head. My main characters, Chrissy and Emma, have just been locked up in the top of a tower by the baddies and I've been trying for ages to figure out how they could escape.

Looking at my eights, I thought how if you turn a figure eight on its side it looks a bit like a set of handcuffs. Handcuffs are pretty strong. If you had enough of them you could join them together and make a chain to climb down the wall. But then I thought, how many would you need? And where could Chrissy and Emma find them?

I chewed at that for a while, and then a brilliant idea came to me. Hey, maybe the baddies could have crates of handcuffs stashed away in the tower? Maybe that's what they were doing — stealing handcuffs and selling them to evil foreign dictators. Like gunrunners, only these baddies would be handcuffrunners and —

That's as far as I got. A finger tapped me on the shoulder. 'Planet Earth calling Sarah,' said Mr Brennan. 'Time for a reality check.'

The whole class rolled about laughing. Mr B. went into his big lecture routine, but luckily he'd only got up to the 'tough world out there,' and 'nobody gives jobs to daydreamers,' when the bell went for lunch and I was saved.

In the playground we talked about the author who was coming. Janina said authors were really rich, so she'd probably wear diamonds and a mink coat. Most of the boys reckoned she'd be a boring old — well, it wasn't very polite, and Jason said, 'I bet she's mean and crabby, with beady eyes like an old witch, and she'll read us pages and pages out of one of her boring old books.'

When we came in after lunch, Mrs Mason was already in the classroom. She didn't look a bit like a witch or a boring old you-know-what. She had glasses and a nice smile and curly, mouse coloured hair that was sort of medium length. I thought she looked a bit like my mum.

Mr Brennan introduced her. 'This is Mrs Mason,' he said. 'She's going to talk to you about writing. Pay attention and you might learn something.' Then he said to her, 'Right, they're all yours then,' and gathered up our maths pads and sat at the table near the window marking them.

Mrs Mason showed us some of her books. Then she showed us a manuscript, so we could see what a book looked like when it was sent to a publisher. I couldn't believe how messy it was. It looked almost like one of my stories. If she'd sent it to Mr Brennan he'd have written NEATNESS!! all over it and given her three out of ten or something. I kept wishing he'd look up and see it, but he didn't. He just kept on marking our maths pads.

After she'd talked to us for a while, Mrs Mason asked if anyone had any questions. Straightaway Jason said 'How much money do you get for being an author?'

I thought she might be angry, but she wasn't. She just laughed and said, 'Yes, that's a very important question, isn't it?' Then she told us that very few children's writers made a living from their books and you had to do it because you loved it.

Janina obviously wasn't listening, because immediately afterwards she asked, 'Do you live in a mansion?'

Everyone went 'Derr,' and Mrs Mason had to explain all over again.

Then Rodney Mills said, 'Have you met any famous authors?' and after everyone had asked, 'have you met' every single author they could think of, Emma Pearson put her hand up and said, 'Where do you get your ideas from.'

'Out of my head,' said Mrs Mason. 'Before you can be a writer on paper, you have to be a writer in your head.'

'What does that mean?' asked Jason. 'How can you be a writer in your head?'

'It means,' said Mrs Mason, 'that you have to be a daydreamer.'

I almost jumped out of my seat. It was like someone had popped a balloon inside my head. Mr Brennan looked up too. He seemed a bit shocked.

'To be a writer,' explained Mrs Mason, 'you need to have exciting adventures inside your head. I spend ninety per cent of my working life daydreaming.'

Everyone giggled.

'Sarah daydreams,' said Janina, and she turned

and looked at me. 'She gets into trouble for it.'

I went bright red, and everyone giggled again.

'So did I,' said Mrs Mason. 'My teachers didn't understand about writing in your head. But the difference between a writer and a daydreamer is that a writer takes the adventures out of her head and puts them down on paper.'

I couldn't believe what I was hearing. I didn't mean to ask a question — I always sound so dumb — but I couldn't stop myself. My hand went up and I said, 'But how come it's always so hard — trying to get the stories out of your head?'

Everyone giggled again and Mr Brennan lifted his head and gave me a 'Sarah, Sarah,' look.

But Mrs Mason was serious, 'That's the most intelligent question I've had all week.' Then she went on, 'It's because when you are writing in your head you are not writing in words. You are writing in pictures and feelings. Words are a writer's tools. They don't only have to have the right meaning, they have to make pictures in readers' minds.'

She picked up a piece of chalk. 'I'll show you what I mean,' she said, and she wrote a word in big letters on the blackboard. Then she said it aloud.

POPOCATAPETL.

'Write that down,' she said. 'Then write down what it makes you think of.'

The class looked blank … 'But I don't know what it means.' said Jason.

'You don't have to. Just tell me what it sounds

like — what it makes you think of.'

'But how can you think of something if you don't know what it is?'

'Try. Shut your eyes and say it and see what comes into your mind.'

I could tell Jason thought that was pretty dumb, but Mr Brennan glared at him so he didn't say anything.

We all shut our eyes. I could see a picture straightaway. 'Popocatapetl,' I said and the picture got clearer and clearer till it was so real I could almost feel it and taste it and smell it. I was only vaguely aware of the rest of the class. Janina was sighing dramatically, like she always does when she thinks she's doing something specially good. Jason was still grumbling to himself. Rodney Mills, who sits behind me, poked me in the back and whispered, 'Popocatapetl is a lake in South America, pass it on,' but I ignored him.

While we were writing, Mrs Mason walked round the room and looked over our shoulders to see how we were going. Sometimes she stopped to talk to people who looked really blank. After a while she said. 'Okay. Everyone seems to have written something. Who'd like to read me what they thought of.'

Straightaway Janina put her hand up. 'POPOCATAPETL reminds me of my pet cat, Misty' she said, and she read out a long description that was full of dorky words like sweet and fluffy and velvety. It wasn't something she'd just thought of. She wrote it a couple of weeks ago for creative writing. Mr Brennan gave her eight out of ten for it and wrote 'Good descriptive words Janina.'

After Janina, Peter Harris put his hand up. He said it sounded like the name of a famous soccer player. Rodney Mills said. 'Popocatapetl is a lake in South America,' and lots of the other kids said 'Yeah, that's what I put, too.'

Mrs Mason laughed. 'I think someone's been cheating,' she said. 'I hate to disappoint you guys, but POPOCATAPETL is actually a mountain, not a lake — a volcano, to be exact.' Then she looked at me. 'Sarah,' she said, 'would you like to read us what you wrote?'

I shook my head. I may be dumb, but I'm not dumb enough to read my work in class. But Mrs Mason persisted. 'Please, Sarah, I'd really like to hear it,' and she wasn't laughing, so somehow, in the end, I found myself standing up. This is what I had written.

POPOCATAPETL

Popocatapetl is a magic word. It makes me think of fireworks. The POPOCATA part is like a whole bunch of them going off one after another ratatatatat, like a machine gun, and the PETL bit is when they burst up in the sky and all the coloured lights come floating down like fairy dust. I don't get to see fireworks very often — only on Australia Day — but now I can have them any time I want. All I have to do is shut my eyes and say POPOCATAPETL.

When I had finished, nobody said anything. Mrs Mason looked at me for a long time. Then she turned to Mr Brennan and she said, 'My friend, you have a writer in your class. Cherish her.'

After that she said, 'Sarah, come up here a minute. I'd like to give you something.' It was one of her books. She autographed it for me and I could hardly speak when I saw what she wrote. 'To Sarah, a writer who understands the magic of words. With best wishes, Angela Mason.'

Mr Brennan looked as if someone had hit him in the mouth with a football. It didn't stop him giving me back my maths pad at the end of school though, and telling me to take it home and finish all the work I hadn't done in class.

All the way home on the bus, my mind was whizzing round like a computer disc. I wrote this story in my head, and after tea I took it out and turned it into words. It took ages. By the time I'd finished it was bedtime, and I'd forgotten about the maths I was supposed to do.

Mr Brennan's going to kill me in the morning, but I don't care any more. And do you know why? Because I'm not a dork after all. I'm a writer. A real author told me so, and to prove it, I've written all across the front of my maths pad, in great big letters:
              POPOCATAPETL.

BIG Weekend

JENNY COOTE

I knew I was in for it as soon as I heard them calling, 'Out the BAAAACCCKK!!!!!' I was already winding myself to make it for the wave hurtling towards me that I was certain would be my link to the Grim Reaper.

I hadn't imagined a wave as big as this and it didn't register. I should have guessed. No one calls out down at Trigg unless they're real kooks, but no kooks were out this Saturday, they were the real scummy SALT worshippers this BIG Saturday.

It was a monstrous, closing out wall and the whole weight of it was coming towards me; no shoulder of the wave to escape to, no Baywatch rescue boat, no nothing. I watched as other surfers gratefully sighed like a barrel collapsing as they dived through the last portion of the chunkiest lip I've ever seen. The easterly had already caught under it and was blowing cold spray off the top of the face onto the retreating surfers.

I didn't know what to do. I was a solitary figure, no one else was anywhere nearby. There would have been relief in getting totally hammered if I had at least been getting totally hammered with somebody else. So I relaxed; so much so that I nearly drowned before the wave hit.

I just fell off my board and did breaststroke. Now the wave seemed to crawl threateningly, almost as if in slow motion, and I felt myself swimming vertically through the water. I thought I might even make it and laughed as I dived in an attempt to avoid the inevitable. I swam about two strokes then felt the powerful surge of the wave pulling me back. I was not going to succumb that easily. I kicked up to the surface just as I felt my leggie somersaulting behind me and grabbed the breath of air I knew I'd have to hold longer than any breath I'd ever held.

The floating, spinning, disorientation was almost enjoyable, before the thumping of the bottom, scraping, breathlessness, panicking, paddling. It was all blurred into one timeless event, even the first rushed breaths of air and the pause before diving under the next wave didn't really register.

I eventually reached the beach and solid, well, hardly moving, ground. I sat for a while, till my legs decided they could stand me up. That's when I realised I had a leggie, but no board. Half of it was on the rocks somewhere near what used to be recognised as Trigg island. Another portion was right in front of the next wave and the last recognisable piece was five metres away, about to turn into a piece of flotsam. I ran to get it; the last part of my $600 Rusty masterpiece.

I could imagine my parents' reaction when they got back from Sydney on Sunday. They were going to hurl! Especially since I had been in real danger of not getting out of trouble this time. I knew from other experiences that my olds had an idea about the strength of the ocean. If I had been a few centimetres further back several tonnes of water would have landed on my head and done the same thing to me as it did to my board. I was already covered in red-tinged cuts and I could tell there were a few decent bruises coming up.

I walked up the hill to the car park. I knew I would have to endure the kilometre walk home but that wasn't the problem. It was the walk up the dune that got me. The names they yelled at me! The gutless kooks, who were too scared to go out there themselves, were making comments about my status as a chick and how that made me unable to catch waves. I don't care if I'm called a kook by someone who can surf and has seen me surf, but when ten-year-old try-hard boogers say things like, *'Stupid bitch, can't even surf,'* and *'Slut, should stay at home where she can do some good,'* I get peeved.

I put up with all their hassling, I always do. The way I was feeling, anything I had to say back would sound feeble anyway. The beautiful comeback lines I did think of came, of course, five hours too late.

When I reached home it was about 8am and I had no idea what to do. Everyone was working and I wanted to avoid the beach, for a few hours at least. So I did what I always do when I am not really hungry but need food to keep me company. I made a nice rich, chocolatey Mississippi Mud Cake, and ate it, all of it. Then I hurled. It was the first time I had eaten till I was sick but it made me feel better, it made me feel as if there was only three hours of a pointless day left to waste. So having expended as much energy as one does by eating such a huge amount of Mississippi Mud Cake, I went to sleep.

I woke about 2 am the next day to an insistent pounding. I hadn't put anything into the cake, so I got up and tried to figure out if it was coming from within me or from outside somewhere. I was wide awake now. Something was definitely trying to get my attention. There was a full moon so I went out onto the balcony and climbed onto the roof. I looked out towards Trigg and nearly slipped on the tiles. Sets were peeling off in the way surfers could only dream of catching in a comp. Perfect barrelling monsters that moved too quickly for any average grommet, catching the wind like it was the air they breathed. Wave after wave holding up and reflecting the moonlight, then cruising effortlessly towards the beach.

It was calling me. I forgot about the carnage of yesterday and thought about unleashing my friend's brother's new stick onto the waves Trigg never gets. The pounding in my head was synchronising my heartbeat with the slamming of that almighty swell down at the sandbanks. The beach I have been down to every day of my life and thought I knew as well as my bedroom, now seemed foreign and unexplored, making me wild with curiosity.

I sat there on the roof for half an hour before I got fidgety in anticipation of daybreak. Then I watched the *Green Iguana* for another half an hour, but inspiration was not what I needed, I already had kicking-butt determination up to my collar bone. I crawled into my wetsuit, trying not to rush in my excitement, grabbed the best of the boards littering our back room and walked as calmly as possible down to the beach. I had plenty of time to waste before it would be light enough to even contemplate going out.

I waited impatiently for an hour or so until there was sufficient light to pick out the beasts of Neptune. As the sun began to peep over the hill, the waves' magnificence was enhanced ten times over and I knew I couldn't last any longer. I was going for a surf.

The water was the warmest it had been in ages because of the Leeuwin current, making me rush even more to feel my whole body rippling in its freedom. The long paddle out was not going to be easy and I had to concentrate. As I looked down the nose of the board and pushed down under the first onslaught of putrid foam, thoughts of the day before started to enter my mind, but I fought them out. I knew if I lingered on my memories I would never go through with this. It was just a matter of turning around and catching the remnants of the waves I really wanted. So I kept on, ignoring the gashes in my legs that had started to throb, as if they knew they could grab my attention enough to send me in.

I made it out past the pressure zone and sat on my board. I sat there for about fifteen minutes just getting the feel for the sets and how the waves were breaking. Gradually more surfers joined me out there. No one looked at anyone else. All eyes were looking towards the horizon, concentrating. There was no doubting that this was a unique day for Trigg.

Some people caught waves and didn't come back out again. Others did but were a lot more subdued. They usually didn't have to paddle far to get back out. It was obvious the waves were breaking fast and unless you were very lucky you were going to get wiped out quickly. There were no whoops of joy, no inflated egos. No one was riding anything well enough to justify behaving the way they do down at Trigg on a normal day.

Then the set I was waiting for came through. It was this or nothing. I let everyone else paddle for the first wave. The cry of someone getting severely wasted reached my ears just before the crunching sound of the lip slamming onto the water below. It put everyone else off, everyone but me.

The initial definition of the wave was unbalanced, it looked too large and I was worried my take-off would be late, but it smoothed out and I went for it, legs, arms, heart and soul. This was my wave, no one else's. The satisfaction, the disappointment, the pain, whatever the result, it was mine.

I felt the pressure behind my board lifting me up and taking any last decisions away from me. I held the board between my hands and swung myself up quickly, already turning to take the right so that the wave wouldn't grab me. There was no time for indecision. That would mean I wouldn't see the sky for three days, until my body floated up to the surface.

I was on my feet, floating, till my board slipped on to the slick surface of the rounding up wave. I turned as tightly as I could without making it feel uncomfortable. Just the thrill of actually making the landing was enough to make me nearly fall off the board. I regained my composure and didn't let my mind wander again.

The ride was fast and as I levelled out its ferociousness was evident, too. I could sense the wave curling around behind me, huge and ominous. I stuck out my hand, running it along the wall on my side, the wake from it just managing to form in time for it to spiral around and crash with the rest of the wave. I slowed back to run level with the edge of the lip and before I knew it I was sitting in the green room. It was moist, very hollow and airless. The breeze that was always there on the surface was blocked out and I felt the comfort of another world. My knees were bent and I was hunched over, but as I realised how big an area I had to inhabit I straightened out and took advantage of an unexplored environment. Breathing the unfamiliar air, feeling its shimmering smoothness, like a watery sleeping bag, tight, secure and comfortable. I slipped deep into the hollow of the wave, realising just in time that if I went any further back I would be locked in. I released the brakes just as the remaining part of the barrel collapsed and spat me out.

I had made it. The ultimate wave. *My* ultimate wave. As I made it into the beach and up the dunes I was oblivious to everything. They may have been cheering at the fence on the dune, they may have been crying. They may not have realised I caught the wave of my life that day at Trigg, but I did.

I remember, without gloating, because no one would believe me.

Glossary

Kook:	Someone who likes to think they can surf, but can't.
SALT:	Surfers Against Lid Traffic, a company started by some Trigg Beach surfers that officially recognised the age-old conflict between stand-up surfers and body boarders.
Leggie:	Leg rope, to avoid losing board.
Rusty:	Surf Company logo.
Chick:	Female of the species.
Boogers:	Body boaders, also referred to as Esky lids, shark bait, speed bumps, etc. etc.
Stick:	Surfboard.
Green Iguana:	Classic surfing video.
Green room:	Surfers' Nirvana.
Set:	Series of three to six waves that comes occasionally and is bigger than average.

An Angel at Cow Town

WARREN FLYNN

'Let's go to Cow Town!'

'Nah, Smith's'll be bedda!'

'Yeah, but we got Pete —'

Pete looked out the games room window. It was sunny and there was a soft easterly. It would be perfect back home at Scabs. Good sized tubes, if there was any swell. And here he was stuck down south, with two cousins talking about him like he was disabled or something.

'Listen, I can surf ya know!'

'Yeah, course Pete, but if you're gunna try a real board …' The left corner of Stir's mouth began to curl.

'Shit, do what ya like, I don't give a …'

'Oh geez, youse two, not again!' Sandy was gettting mad. 'Look, I thought we agreed. Pete do you want to try my old board or not?'

Pete didn't know. He wanted to say 'Yes' to

Sandy, but 'No' to Stir. Why were cousins invented? Last year, when he came to Perth with Auntie Alison, Stir stuffed up their CD player. In his own house, he was even worse. If Peter took his boogie board, he would drop in on every one of Stir's bloody waves.

'Nahh ...' he could see Stir's lip curling again.

'Afraid of heights tea bag?'

'LOOK, DROP IT I SAID!' Sandy moved towards him.

Stir was too fast. The fly screen door slapped and bounced shut before she was near him. Sandy shook her head.

'Look, we'll take it anyway. It's no big deal. If you change your mind, it's there. You can decide when we get there, okay?'

Pete nodded. He felt like a fool. As the screen door smacked shut again, he could see her heading to the garage. From behind, she looked just like a guy. Big biceps and shoulders like a Chinese swimmer.

In the car, it felt hot already. Pete could see the little dust particles, shining like Tinker Bell in front of the cracking plastic of the Falcon's dash. The vinyl smelt musty and sweaty. He checked his watch. They'd only been driving twenty minutes. He felt prickly and sticky between his legs, even without his wetty. Uncle Mike might have had a point about his speedos. Two days earlier, when they were all down at the bay, Stir's Dad laughed when he saw Stir and him swimming in their boardies and T-shirts.

'You scared of getting wet or something? Might as well go swimming in a tux!'

At least they kept the stingers off.

Pete wondered what his mum and Auntie Ali were doing. Mum always wanted to come down south. She knew he hated Stir, but there was no point in protesting. She just went all quiet. He hated that even more than her shouting. She reckoned she'd move down south if the firm had an office. She'd never mentioned it until Dad moved out.

Sandy hit the brakes as they dropped over a crest, and swerved the old sedan across the big open intersection. Cowaramup flashed by on the signpost so fast that Peter only caught the first three letters: C-O-W.

It was bumpy and narrow. Sandy turned up the radio some more, because of the thumping from the tyres. It was a re-hash of an old Bob Dylan song about knocking on heaven's door. Peter recognised it from one of his mum's old cassettes.

In the back, Stir was trying to hum along. He sounded terrible. Pete turned around. Stir looked pathetic. His mouth all twisted up like a crushed Coke can, he was doing disgusting hand movements, miming the guitar solo. It was hard to believe he was only one year younger.

'ALISTAIR!' Sandy never called him that unless she was losing it.

Scrubby peppermints were growing right up to the verge. Navy blue shadows flashed by. Now and then one would whip the rear view mirror. Pete wound down his window a little more. He could smell the ocean, but ahead there was nothing but the thin grey strip of road. The olive-green bush on each side, and here and there, small lumps of limestone poking out of the sand like pieces of old shipwrecks.

'Very far now?'

'Just a few more k's,' Sandy sighed.

A few hills later and there it was. The dark curve of the ocean, and halfway to the horizon, the white teeth of reefs. Immediately in front of them, two points drew a huge 'U', about two kilometres across. Closer to the crescent of the white shoreline, the deeper indigo shallowed and softened into shining emerald. From each side of the bay, the water was creased by the moving smiles of even swells. There were breaks off each of the points, and like forgotten Lego pieces, coloured shapes of surfers were scattered across the bay.

'Wow!' Pete gasped.

'Yeah, looks good doesn't it,' Sandy grinned.

'Bit small,' whined Stir.

The road wound down past the toilets and the thatched shelters of a little beach opposite the deli. There were a few mums in bikinis and toddlers running around with T-shirts and no pants.

Pete could see it had probably been a quiet fishing spot once. Now rooftops nudged peppermints aside and windows outshone the yellow limestone outcrops. And there, squatting halfway up the hill, was a little building with a cross on top. It reminded him of something he'd seen about Greece. But the houses were different. There were grey old fibro shacks, and overlooking them, two-storey brick places, with huge panels of smoked glass and BMs and Mercs out the front. One big Merc looked long enough to be a stretch. Shining and black like a hearse.

It was mid-week, but even so, the car park near the southern point was half full. Mostly old vans and wagons. One guy, older than Pete's Mum, was sitting on the tailgate of a Kingswood with a toothbrush in one hand, and a can of VB in the other. He looked a mess. He was wearing footy shorts and a dirty sleeping bag draped around leathery shoulders. His hair was a bleached and matted tangle. He stared at them as they took the boards off the roof rack, his eyes following Sandy as she threw the ockies in the back.

Out of the car it felt cool, despite the cloudless sky. There was a steady light offshore breeze, but it was still early, and Pete shivered as he peeled off his shirt and zipped up his wetty. He decided he'd give Sandy's board a try. Stir would rubbish him anyway. At least down here, no one he knew would see him. And he mightn't get another chance.

'Sure you can lift it?' Stir mocked, screwing up his face.

'Piss off!' hissed Sandy.

'Yours need any, Pete?' She held out the block of wax.

Pete examined the deck. He wasn't sure. There

was still a lot of old stuff on, turned to a rust colour from dust. Sandy could see him frowning. She swung the board towards her, running her long fingers across the surface.

'Looks all right,' she flicked back her long hair and smiled. 'You right with the ankle strap?'

'Yeah, course.' The rubber was perished, and the velcro frayed, but it still seemed to hold okay.

The board was light, but it was hard keeping balance as they made their way across the round, smooth, dark rocks leading to the water's edge. Too small to stand on and too big to straddle, they wobbled with every step. By the time Pete had reached the water, Stir was already fifty metres out, paddling fluidly off to the left, by the reef. Pete couldn't see any rips. Just big lumps of weed-covered reef sticking out like dribbling sea monsters on the left side. Further out, two boogie boarders, flippers churning, were cutting right to beat a break. There were probably about a dozen board riders, their wetsuits glistening in the low-angled sun. Beautifully even sets, about two to two and half metres high, were sliding in off the point. Sandy had slowed down, turning now and then, waiting for him. He caught up when she reached the water.

'You gunna be okay?' she asked.

'Yeah, sure.'

'Orright, well just take it easy to start with. There's a couple of rocks just under the surface over there. Just stick to left-handers and you'll be fine.'

'Yeah, okay.'

Sandy slapped her board down on the clear water.

'The car's locked, so if you want your other stuff,' she slid onto her deck and started paddling, 'you'll have to flag me down.'

By the time Pete had his board in the water, she was already ten metres away, her right toe pointed and flicking up in rhythm to her smooth, strong strokes.

It felt funny to be surfing in bare feet, after years of boogie-boarding with flippers. And so far out of the water too! He felt exposed, but it sure made paddling easier, even though he couldn't keep up with Sandy.

The water was so clean! Below him, he could see anemones waving their orange arms like pom pom girls in slo mo. He paddled faster over the dark weed. He hated how the sea grass always made strange shapes suddenly appear. He was glad to lift up over the first wash. Sandy's light blue suit was going up over the lip of larger wave further out. Pete paddled fast, over to the left, trying to beat the next swell before it broke. He was feeling more confident now, working hard with both arms and willing himself along, using his legs for leverage. He could see the turquoise and the paler green looming. Rearing in front of him as the water shallowed, he could feel his board lifting under him as the wave peaked. Two more strokes with all he had. He pushed and ducked his head. The wave curled and broke behind him. He shook the water from his hair. His arms were already aching and he could feel his heart pumping against the fibreglass deck of the board.

Suddenly, he sensed something behind him. He heard a 'Whoosh!' Before he could turn, there was a shape. Another board.

'G'day,' the surfer grunted, as he skimmed by.

Pete, adrenaline racing, couldn't respond. The other guy was already metres away. No wetsuit, and matted hair, a wet smokey-gold. The guy from the car park.

Then there was a wall of white wash. Instinctively, Pete dived deep. He felt the tug on his leg rope as his board took the wash. He popped back into the bright air, sucking it in as he scrambled back onto the deck. Further out, he could see Sandy, crouching low under a folding tube. Charging through, then snapping it up and over the lip, before it closed out.

Directly in front, a good-sized swell was looming. If he was fast, he could make it. He sat up and spun the board, craning his neck around to time his approach. Then he was down, paddling fast, leaning forward as he felt the surge under him. Lifting up and forward. He was nearly there! Arms aching he willed the board forward. But he was too late, and he felt the whip of salt in his face as the wave passed below him.

He turned to see a larger wave breaking in front. Screaming down its face was Stir, carving an arrow of silver across the green wall. He was yelling something. Pete only caught, 'Sucker!' before he plunged deep again. The dark green around him, the jerk of the leg rope on his ankle.

The fizz of sparkling bubbles in the emerald water. Lungs bursting, he lunged for the surface. If only he'd had his boogie board!

Back up and paddling again Sandy was only thirty or so metres away now. And there was that old guy, astride his board, next to her. Across to the right he could see Stir, paddling out fast, in the lull between sets. Beneath him, Pete watched dark shapes again. Just weed? But it was moving in the wrong direction!

SHARK! He tried to yell, but nothing would come out.

Before he could even start paddling, he saw its wings, and flumped onto his board. It was a big ray. A grey flag flapping away in slow motion towards the reef.

Pete felt the surge of water being sucked towards him and intuitively paddled fast as he felt the wave gathering under him. He was on it! On one knee! Standing! Flying! Fantastic! Down the face. He felt the nose dip. Wipe out!

Unreal! He broke the surface grinning. He wanted to yell out to Sandy, but she was paddling out further, to a larger break out the back. He didn't even mind Stir whizzing by on the next wave, laughing.

In the next set, Pete caught another. And this time, he remembered to turn. But he cut back too severely and went over the falls backwards. The one after, a smaller wave, he rode well, crouching low, grabbing the rails only at the last second.

More relaxed with every set, he was judging them well, managing at least one reasonable ride for each wipe-out. As the wind picked up, the size increased and they were hollowing out more. Building up and tubing into long pipe-lines, or closing out suddenly. Over to the left, Stir was taking a right-hander, charging through the tube and cutting back sharply, as a lump of reef reared in front of him.

Though he was positioned well, Pete thought the next one was too small. He could see the dark blue line of a much larger one gathering out the back. He turned and began paddling slowly to build momentum. He could feel the water sucking back. He increased his speed. He felt cold as the swell's height shadowed him. He could feel the air rushing up as he pushed down its steepening slope. He was on it! Surging forward! Up fast! Have to turn! Up! Fantastic! Down the face! Slicing sideways, leaning back. Nose up. Nose up! Yelling. His voice! Tube closing! Left foot wobble! Wipe-out! Sideways into the wall and over the falls! Go deep! Deep. The tug on his leg rope, then nothing. Like a salmon on a whiting line. He could feel the bracelet of velcro on his ankle. Long swim. Got to get up. Light. Fizz of foam. Air! Gasping. A shadow.

Another wave. Close mouth. A crunch and splinter of fibreglass on his skull. His front tooth chipping. That must have hurt, he thought, then … BLACK.

Someone has a fist in my stomach. Pushing up and up and I'm going to burst. Open. It's out.

Warm and sweet. There's a dog panting. Panting. There's little diamonds on the rock here. They're so tiny. Moaning. God! Thank God! Feet wet and shiny. Jesus! Sandy's painted toe nail. Panting. Will he be all right. Pete. Pete?!

The cool. The dark is better ... hospital better ... Peter? Will he be okay? Can they see the diamonds? Geez, poor kid. Okay, Okay. Moaning. Who's moaning? Geez. The cut's not bad, but he'll need stitches ... Ohhhh. Hey it's you. It's you moaning. Bright! There's fingers on my throat. Stir? What's that rattling sound? Stir, can you hear that rattling? Pairs of feet listening. Pulse is settling down ... should be okay, keep that shirt on the cut — BRIGHT. What ugly toes — the car ... yep, that's it. Geez listen to his teeth, would ya. I'm floating. This feels good, but my tooth hurts. What's that sound? BRIGHT!

Bare-feet and gravel. The car park. That's it, ease him in. Musty smell. Warm bread smell. No. No, leave his suit on, put the blanket over him, yeah ... that's normal ... just in shock. Pete? That's Stir. Pete? Sandy. PETER! Who's that? BRIGHT! Brown face, golden hair.

'G'day.'

The old guy. Someone's groaning.

'Hey, stay awake a minute!'

'PETER!'

His head is all sunlight. Warm fingers on my neck.

'Pete, wriggle your left fingers will ya. Yeah! Great!'

My tooth is sharp. It hurts. Groaning.

'Now, your right toes. Feel my fingers on this foot? Wriggle your toes. That's it! Great!'

Warm arm around me. Soft.

'That's it, you stay with him. I'll stick your boards on. His pulse has settled down heaps. He'll need hospital though. Could call an ambulance, but by the time they get organised, you'd be there I reckon. There's no danger. Not too much blood gone. Margaret would be the closest. You know the way? Peter, how are you feeling? Come on, talk to me!'

My mouth hurts, but it's warm in the back seat.

'Hey, Peter! Come on man, you can hear me, talk to me. How do you feel?'

'Pretty sore.' Sound drunk.

'Yeah, that's normal. You'll be all right. Back in the surf in no time. Thanks to your mate.' It was Stir holding him.

'He's …' come on talk … 'he's my cousin.'

'Well, I reckon he's your mate now. Heh?' Closing the door gently, pushing it till it locked.

'Sure you'll be okay?' the old guy asked. Pete wasn't sure. His tooth hurt.

'Yeah,' Sandy replied, 'if you're sure …'

'Yep, he'll be fine. Just concussed.'

'Look … I don't know …'

'Ahh … I wouldn't have been able to do anything without you two. Your little brother was so quick! Without him holding him up … And you got him in fast! Made all the difference.'

'But the mouth to mouth …'

'Yeah … well, I'm glad he's okay.'

'Where did you learn all that stuff? Are you a doctor?'

'Nah,' he laughed. 'Used to teach Phys. Ed. once. Anyway, better get him to Margaret River fairly soon, I reckon …'

'Yeah.'

The car cranked and throbbed into life.

'Thanks!' Stir yelled as they backed up.

'Hey!' Sandy called out through the window. 'What's your name?'

'Round here they call me Fizz … or sometimes, Feral.'

'See ya!'

'Bye!'

Pete could hear him chuckling as they moved onto the road and picked up speed.

Dallas' Dad

KIM SCOTT

Dallas was a friend of mine who liked hurting people. I never said it as clearly as that when I knew him and maybe it's not exactly true, because sometimes he tried to stop himself. But mostly, if something was going wrong for him, you'd see a particular expression come onto his face and next thing you knew some kid would be holding their face and crying and Dallas would be standing to one side, trying not to look too pleased with himself.

He was a small, wiry boy who hid beneath his baseball cap so that most people never saw his face except when he was fighting, or about to fight. And then he was very quick, and ruthless with his fists and feet.

I first met him when I started at a new school. I had recently moved in with my uncle and aunty. Their children were all younger than me, and so I felt like the odd one out. People were always dropping in to visit or stay with us, and they were always related in some way or another to my cousins. Of course, that meant they were also related to me, but I didn't know anything about them. Unc used to explain it all, to me and to the visitors, how we fitted in together. Sometimes I felt them slyly studying me, and I used to worry about what was the best way to act.

I had only been living there for a short time before we all shifted house. 'We have to get away,' Unc said. 'We need to make a bit of space for ourselves.'

So it was my first day at the new school.

'You'll have to sit beside Dallas,' said the teacher. I remember wondering why she looked so concerned. It was obvious that the only vacant seat in the classroom was the one next to the kid she called Dallas.

I suppose he was sitting on his own because of the way he was, you know.

As I sat down he put his left elbow on the desk like a barrier between us, and rested his head on his left hand, with his face turned away from me. He was writing or drawing something with his other hand. I couldn't tell what it was.

You gotta realise, I wasn't at my best. I didn't feel very happy, or very strong. I'd broken my arm a couple of days before, but because it wasn't my writing arm Unc wouldn't let me stay home. So not only was I still getting used to my new family, but here I was in another house, another suburb, another school, another classroom.

Another desk. 'Oh well,' I thought, trying to cheer myself up, 'it's a chance to make new friends.' I glanced across at Dallas. He was colouring a wooden ruler with black ink. The teacher's name was written on the ruler in small neat letters, and Dallas just kept moving his pen until there was nothing but black, and no name at all.

It was just before lunch, and I was nervous about what it would be like in the playground. I didn't know anyone. What would I do? Who would I play with? Would anyone speak to me? I tried to psyche myself up, like Unc had said. I wanted to be positive, to make the best of things. I asked Dallas if I could use his pen.

I won't tell you what he said to me. At the time I didn't even really understand what he meant, but I knew it was nasty. Let's just say he said, 'Lick my bum.'

And I said something like, 'You can jam your pen up yours, and then lick my bum.'

That was the first time I saw his face take on that particular expression it had. I saw his face change, saw his eyes boring into mine, but I never saw his fist coming.

So there I was, crying. Yeah, I was crying. Shame. I was only a kid, crying in front of the whole class like that. Me and him both got busted, put in what the school called Isolation for a couple of days. And when they found out Dallas had stolen all the teacher's gear — pens, ruler, the works — he got into even more trouble. His mum was called to the school. We heard her shouting and screaming in the school office, and the story was she grabbed the principal by the throat. Then Welfare came sniffing around Dallas' family's door. Unc said the school did it all wrong, and yeah Dallas was a violent little kid but Unc reckoned that his family had enough trouble on their plate right now. 'Don't worry if the school tells you off, you just don't let him bully you. But, really, that's the only way he knows. You just be cleverer than him.'

I dunno how me and Dallas got to be friends. He used to come around to my place, and Unc would help him fix his bike, stuff like that. We had a space at the end of the driveway where Unc kept his tools, and there was a bench he used to sit on, sometimes, and play guitar. In my mind's eye I can still see him there, gazing down the driveway at the old trees in the shabby little park which began across from our house.

Dallas was always quiet when he was around Unc. He'd watch him working, even when we were playing together. He used to study the details of what Unc did; like where the tools were put, and even where and when and how Unc wiped his hands. Unc used to talk as he was doing things, too. 'Now, we're gunna need that big spanner,' or 'Well, I wonder how I'm gunna do this? Maybe I could …' Unc talked softly like that all the time. When we got older some of us used to laugh at the way he did it, but probably, if you paid attention like Dallas did, you could learn a lot.

I remember making fun of Dallas once for the way he watched Unc so closely, and all he did was smile and shrug. We must have been friends by then, unna?

Another time we were doing jumps over an earth ramp we'd made in the park, and the chain on Dallas' bike broke. Dallas stepped back from the bike, held his chin in one hand, and looked thoughtfully at the suddenly useless piece of machinery. 'Hmm,' he went. He looked just like Unc. I laughed at him, but not for long, because he got wild. I supposed it was easier to get wild than to try and fix the bike, or to admit that he couldn't. I leapt on my own bike, and stayed out of reach until he'd calmed down. He was only a little kid, but by then I knew how he got when he was angry.

I must have been accident prone that year, because I was on crutches the time Unc gave Dallas his own bike to use. Dallas had always wanted to use that bike. Unc kept it hanging on the wall. We used to flick the wheels sometimes, just to see how long they kept spinning. The wheel would stop, eventually, for just an instant, and then rotate back the other way. We would watch and wait as it rotated one way, then the other, again and again, each rotation smaller than the one before it until, finally, the valve came to a halt at the very top centre of the rim.

Unc let me have a little ride on that bike once. It glided along so smoothly it was as if you always had the wind behind you. It looked good just hanging on the wall. It had chrome bits on it, and I reckoned the crankset and pedals looked like jewellery.

Unc said to Dallas, 'What about you take my bike and go look for those boys.' It was his own kids, my cousins, that he wanted to come home. When I write down what he said, it looks like a question, but it wasn't. It wasn't an order either. Dallas said, 'What, take that?' and, lifting his chin, he pointed his lips at Unc's bike. You could see he was keen to ride it, and he gave a big grin before closing himself up once again. Unc told him to take care because there was a little problem working its gears. As he rolled away Dallas was looking at the shadow he and the bike cast on the ground, and he seemed to be dancing on the pedals.

My cousins had been home for a long time and it was coming on dark when we saw Dallas. At first he was just a tiny figure in the distance and gloom beneath the trees at the centre of the park. He was pushing Unc's bike, and as he came up the grassy slope he was leaning so hard into it that my cousins could see there was something wrong.

'How come he's got your bike, Dad?'

'Look, there's something wrong with it.'

'He stacked it, unna?'

I could tell there was something wrong with Dallas, too. He was even more slumped than usual, and although he had the sort of complexion on which it was hard to see tear smudges, they were there all right. The whites of his eyes were red, and he was bruised, and there were grazes on his knees and elbows.

'What happened?'

He kept his eyes on the bike, and on his own limbs as he turned and twisted to show us his abrasions and blood.

'I blacked out,' he said. 'I was going down a hill, and I blacked out. I must've blacked out. I woke up and I was just lying in the road, and the bike was next to me.' His voice was hoarse, a damaged whisper.

Unc put his arm around Dallas and pushed the bike across to his sons. I was hobbling along behind them and I saw how Dallas leaned into Unc's side. It looked sort of funny, because Unc was only a short man himself. 'I think maybe the derailleur got jammed in the spokes, and threw you off, knocked you out,' said Unc.

Unc made Dallas get into the car with us, even though he said he didn't need a lift. I thought he was just being polite because he knew how Unc hated to use the car unless he was going a long way. But now I think he meant it, and if we hadn't given him a lift it might have turned out differently. Then again, the only difference might have been that I didn't go with them, and then I wouldn't have understood how it all happened.

We pulled into Dallas' place, and Unc drove around a car that was parked across the end of the drive and parked close to the front door so that Dallas wouldn't have to walk very far. Dallas' mum came running out of the house before we had even turned off the motor. 'Oh, Dallas …' she called, rushing to the passenger door. Her face was bruised and red, as if she'd also had a crash. 'That's funny,' I thought. 'They both got hurt the same day.'

She was shaking, and fumbling, and rushing so much to get Dallas out of the car that she made everything more difficult for him. Dallas pushed her away, and when she looked up and saw Unc standing at the front door of the house something happened to her face.

'Thanks Steven,' she said to my uncle, her voice all dry and cold. 'Thanks, but we'll be right now.'

Unc wasn't one to be rushed, but this time he seemed particularly slow and calm. He was trying to explain what he'd thought had happened, and even I could tell that Dallas's mum didn't want to listen, and just wanted him to leave. Dallas was standing in the doorway, following their awkward conversation, and now and then glancing into the house.

A man stepped out, and grabbed Dallas by the arm. He was a big man, and he went to push past Unc, dragging Dallas behind him. 'Hang on a bit,' said Unc, and he put his hand out. The man turned away from Unc, and cuffed Dallas around the head. 'Get in the car.' And then Dallas' mum had fallen over, and I thought the man was bending to help her up, but he suddenly swung around and king-hit Unc. Unc went over the edge of the steps, and landed on his back in the weedy little garden.

I was still sitting in the car, with one crutch out the door. The man stumbled on it as he rushed past, and swore, and tried to slam the door on me but the crutch stopped it. He leapt in the car behind us, with Dallas shouting and swearing at him. The car took off with its tyres squealing and smoking, and the stink of burnt rubber kept growing stronger and stronger. Unc was sitting in the dirt, leaning back on his arms, and shaking his head. Blood was dripping onto his shirt, and Dallas' mum was curled up on her side and sobbing.

They crashed not far from home. I never heard an explosion, but I think I remember an ambulance siren. They said Dallas wasn't wearing a seat belt, and was crushed between the steering wheel and his father.

Bitten by the Millennium Bug

ELAINE FORRESTAL

The man on the path was massive! Rolls of fat bulged out at the neck and rippled between the buttons of his old-fashioned coat. His pale-dough face looked as if it had been squashed straight onto his pudgy shoulders. On the top of his head a thin patch of straight fair hair lay like dead grass. Two small round eyes stared out over fat cheeks and a long scar twisted his mouth into a permanent scowl.

I wanted to run. Back to Mum and Aunt Oona and Grannie. Back to the safety of the farmhouse, sheltering in the drumlin folds below the Mountains of Mourne. But I'd already given up trying to find the way. I'd been walking for hours.

'Tis late for a wee girl like yourself to be out now,' the voice rumbled. The man rolled towards me. I tried to back away, but my feet seemed to be stuck.

While his eyes searched around and behind me, the man said, 'Y're on your own, then?'

'Connan is with me!' I said, trying not to sound scared. 'He's not far away.' I took a step backwards, but stumbled on the rough path.

'Australian?' the man frowned. I quickly folded my arms across the Perth Western Australia logo on my windcheater but my accent had already given me away.

The black shape of the man towered over me. His voice grated and rattled like loose stones down a steep path. 'And what would be bringin' y' all the way to Northern Ireland?' I was shivering with cold and fright, but I still couldn't run. My legs wouldn't move.

I was wishing I'd listened to Mum. She had warned me that Connan was a real handful. But I couldn't bear to be shut up in the house a minute longer. 'Please!' I begged. 'I won't go far. I promise!' Mum had looked at her sister, Oona. 'Och, she'll come to no harm,' Oona said. 'And the dog could surely do with a walk.'

Since Grampa died, nothing in the family had been normal. Grannie hardly came out of her room. Mum and Aunt Oona drank endless cups of coffee and poor Connan had been almost forgotten. I tried to keep out of everyone's way, but it was cold and misty outside and we hadn't had time to pack games and stuff. We took the first flight out of Perth after Mum got the news. So Aunt Oona found some rope and made up a sort of collar and lead for Con. 'Y're grannie has no need of such things,' she said, slipping the rope around his neck. 'They understand each other, so they do. Mind you, she does take him out of a mornin'. Before he's been fed.' Aunt Oona's eyes twinkled for the first time in days.

'But I'll go crazy if I have to wait till morning!' I told her. 'Aye, would I could get out for a wee while meself,' Oona sighed. 'But if y' hold tight to this rope here, y'll manage him all right.'

Connan was really excited about going out. He bounced around all over the place, wagging his whole body. When he bounded towards the door the rope pulled tight. We all laughed at the surprised look on his face.

I ran with him to the top of the hill. When he stopped and snuffled curiously under a thick clump of bushes, I looked out over the rolling fields with their thin black lines of hedges and dry stone walls. I just stood there taking big breaths of fresh air. It was great to be out. To get away from the heavy atmosphere of mourning that filled the house. I was sad about Grampa, but I didn't really know him very well. It was always Grannie who wrote letters and sent presents for Christmas and birthdays.

When Connan had finished checking out the wildlife he took off again, down into the valley. He knew where he was going and I was happy to follow. But when he dived under a hedge at the edge of the woods his rope snagged. Con gave a sharp tug and twisted his head. Suddenly I had his lead in my hand, but no dog. I called to him to come back, but he had his nose down and his body stretched out full length. He was not stopping for anyone. I had to get down on my knees and squeeze through the hedge to run after him. But the more I ran and called to him, the deeper into the woods he went. I could see the white tip of his tail waving among the trees and bracken for a while. Then he disappeared. The high-pitched yodelling sound that he had inherited from his hunting ancestors was all that was left for me to follow.

I knew I was a long way from the farmhouse. But I didn't dare go back to Grannie's without Con. I picked my way through the damp woods, trying not to panic. Thorny bushes scratched and stung my hands. My shoes and the legs of my jeans were soaked from running through the damp undergrowth. My throat was sore from calling. It was getting dark and I was hopelessly lost.

When I saw a light blinking through the trees, I ran towards it. I did not see the man waiting in the shadows.

His eerie, almost colourless eyes were sunken into the flesh of his misshapen face. His body was enormous — like a hot-air balloon anchored to the ground by impossibly small feet and legs. He stood so close his huge bulk blocked out the light. 'So?' he said. He was waiting for an answer. 'My grandfather died,' I gulped. 'Ahhh,' the sound sighed slowly out of his twisted mouth. 'That he did.'

'Did you know him?' Suddenly a small ray of

hope flickered under the heavy dread that had settled on my chest. 'I did of course,' the man said. 'Oh, then you could phone my Grannie's house. Tell them where I am.' The words tumbled out.

'No!' Rolls of flesh wobbled around his neck as he shook his head. 'Never owned a telephone,' he barked. 'Noisy, intrusive things, drapin' their great ugly wires all over the countryside.' I shrank back inside my windcheater, wishing I had Mum's mobile with me. A wet cotton wool feeling was rising in my throat.

Then I heard it! A high-pitched whine. 'That's Connan!' I gasped. Desperately I pushed past the man and ran towards the sound. 'Come back here!' he yelled as he followed me up the path.

The whining sound was coming from behind a high stone wall beside the house. In the wall was a wooden gate. I pushed. The gate rattled, but didn't open. Connan whined again as I groped inside a small opening and lifted the latch. The gate swung inwards just as the man lumbered up beside me.

I flung my arms around Connan's neck and held him close. 'How did you get in here, you wicked dog!' But I was so pleased to see him that I couldn't be angry. At first I didn't take any notice of the shoe he held in his mouth. I looked up at the man. His scarred face was even more ghastly in the glimmer of light that reached us from the window of the house. He closed the gate firmly behind him and stood in front of it. I was trapped in the walled garden. My stomach churned and I felt the panic rising again. Then more light flooded across the tangled shrubs and narrow pathway. The man moved towards it. I turned my head and saw a woman standing in the open doorway of the house.

'Och, Roseanne. I told y' not to let him anywhere near the cellar,' the man grumbled. 'Now we'll have to keep the wee girl as well.'

'Y' can't be serious, Eamon. Y'll have the whole county out searchin'. For The Dear's sake just go to the police. Tell them what happened.'

The round head shook furiously. 'Y' know well what they think o' me,' the man said.

'Sure and there's no way you are to blame for that beatin' y' took; the trauma that's left y' seekin' comfort in food …'

'Try tellin' them that,' he rumbled.

'Aye! I will! And I'll ask them why they've done nothin' to stop thugs and muggers roamin' our streets. Nothin'! In all these years …'

While they were busy arguing, I tried to take the shoe from Connan's mouth. He wouldn't give it up. But as I tugged at it, I realised that it was not really a shoe. It was a heavy farmer's boot. A boot very like one that still lay, caked with mud, in Grannie's back porch. It had the same deeply worn crease across the middle that Grampa's left boot always had. It came from constantly walking on the ball of his foot because his left leg was a good two inches shorter than his right.

I managed to ease the rope back over Connan's head, in spite of the boot in his mouth. Something very strange was going on. Something that made me even more desperate to get away from there. I looked around. Inching slowly back towards the gate, I tried to remember the layout of the fields. There must be other houses with their lights on by now. I knew I could easily outrun the man — and probably the woman, too. Even if I couldn't get back to Grannie's, I had to tell someone that my grandfather had been murdered after all. No one wanted to believe that such an evil thing could happen in the tiny, tight-knit, farming community. But silently, in their hearts, and whispering behind their hands, everyone was saying that William McNaught had not leapt naked from the top of the steepest bluff in the Mournes. He was pushed.

'Y're as daft as the day y' were born, Eamon Riley.' The woman said, raising her voice as she strode out of the house. 'And what were the pair o' y' doin' up there on the mountain anyroad? There's Will, Dear love 'im, with his gammy leg and you weighin' half a ton. Neither of y' fit to be walkin' a hundred yards, let alone climbin' up there!' She stood, hands on hips, glaring at Eamon. Without warning the man's huge bulk sagged under the weight of her words. He seemed to fold in on himself as if someone had pulled out the stopper from a blow-up doll.

I took another step towards the gate. I was reaching for the latch when Roseanne leapt across in front of me, blocking my way.

'Let me out!' I screamed. At last the panic I was trying not to show exploded inside me. 'You can't keep me here! My mother will be worried.

They'll all come looking for me. And for Con. I'll scream and scream until they find me!' I lashed out at the woman, pummelling her chest and shoulders with my free hand and clinging desperately to Con with the other. The dog barked, tugging at the rope. But Roseanne stood perfectly still, accepting the blows to her body as if they were no more nor less than she expected.

When I finally stopped, limp and exhausted, Roseanne said, 'And why would we be wantin' t' keep a young wildcat like y'rself? We're decent folk, Eamon and me. Everyone thinks ill of him for the way he looks. But it's no fault of his!'

'That's Grampa's boot!' I said accusingly. I didn't know what to think about Eamon and the way he looked. Con clamped his teeth even tighter around the battered leather boot and looked knowingly from me to Roseanne. If only he could talk. Maybe he knew exactly how Grampa died. He was Grannie's dog, but you couldn't put on a coat in her back porch without Con appearing from nowhere, wagging his tail and begging to be taken for a walk. Had he gone out with Grampa that night and come home alone? Had he tried to tell them — get them to follow him? But been shut in. Trapped by their grief. He did seem to head straight for Eamon's house, as soon as he slipped his lead.

'It is Will's boot,' Roseanne said sadly. 'And the rest of his clothes are here, too. When Connan appeared in the yard I ran my eyes around the weathered stones and solid gate that enclosed the garden. 'He has a hole under the wall that he always uses,' The woman answered my unspoken question. 'Eamon went out to wait on the path. I think he expected your grandmother. He told me to keep Con in, upstairs. But the dog was frantic. He would have clawed his way right through that cellar door, so he would. Anyway, it's no use tryin' t' hide these things. It will only be worse for Eamon in the end.'

By then, a soft, gulping sound was coming from the huge body of Eamon, now slumped on the garden bench. Roseanne made a move towards him, then remembered she was guarding the gate. 'Och, away t' your mother, then.' She lifted her arms in a gesture of resignation and went to comfort the man who was blowing his nose loudly. I stood there, not knowing what to do. Suddenly I felt sorry for both Eamon and Roseanne. But I needed to know what was going on. How had my Grampa died? Why was Eamon afraid to go to the police? My family was in shock. But I could see now that this odd looking man had also been damaged. Had he killed Will McNaught? Somehow I could no longer imagine him doing it.

Roseanne bent over Eamon and put her arm around his shoulder. He sat like a sack of beans on the stone garden seat under the window. I left the gate and moved closer to hear what they were saying.

'He was my friend.'

'Y' were always feudin'.'

Eamon nodded. 'Since we were six years old,' he said. 'It was the way we were.' He lifted his head and stared into the sky. The moon shone briefly through a chink in the clouds, silhouetting the mountains. 'We left the pub together, well after closin'. The crack was great that night — like old times. We were laughin', jokin' about the daft buggers bookin' tickets to watch the dawn of the new millennium in Antarctica, New Zealand, Australia ...' He looked across at me. 'I told Will he should go and visit his daughter, but he said she was on the wrong edge of the country. "Y' need an eastern edge," he said. "And mountains —" like these here. He got very excited. Said we could make ourselves a fortune at the turn of the century. We walked and talked and drank more whiskey from the bottle he was carryin' home. Next thing I know we're in the Mournes. Trippin' and slidin' and laughin' fit to bust a gut. Then he stumbles. Right on the edge. I grab for him —'

'God save us, Eamon, what ever possessed y'?'

Eamon looked at Roseanne and drew in a dreadful, shuddering breath that caused his flesh to heave and settle. 'We were checkin' out the best place to watch the sunrise. The first dawn of the new age Will said. Then he was gone.' Eamon's head dropped to his flabby chest. 'By the time I scrambled down to him, he was dead. I couldn't lift him. So I sat with him a while. Later I thought, they'll say I pushed him. They won't believe me. So I took his clothes. And covered him with bracken to keep him warm. I thought, if they ever found him, they wouldn't know who he was — without his clothes.'

There was a dreadful silence. Roseanne's body

stiffened. She took her arm from Eamon's shoulder. One hand went up and covered her mouth. She stood like a statue; not breathing. I thought she must be having some sort of fit. 'Are you all right?' I asked. She turned, nodding her head, and I saw that she was laughing.

'I'm so sorry,' Roseanne gasped, bending almost double to control her laughter. 'I know it's a terrible tragedy, but can y' imagine those two eedjits, puffin' up the mountain before dawn — in the middle o' winter — to look at a sunrise? The telephone is too modern for Eamon and Will was still cuttin' his grass with a scythe! They're the last two people on earth you'd expect to be bitten by the millennium bug!' She laughed freely for several seconds, then stopped abruptly. 'We've all lost a friend,' she said, looking from Eamon to me. 'But long faces will never bring him back. Sometimes y' just have to laugh or you'd spend your whole life cryin'.' She fished one hand into her sleeve, pulled out a handkerchief and wiped her eyes.

Eamon stared at her. Then slowly his twisted mouth turned up on one side. His pale eyes lit up and a lovely, chuckling sound rocked his mountainous body like an earthquake. That's when I started to giggle. I couldn't help it.

Biographical Notes

Margot Bosonnet started writing when her children grew up. She is the author of *Skyscraper Ted and Other Zany Verse* and of the much-loved Red Belly trilogy: *Up the Red Belly, Red Belly, Yellow Belly* and *Beyond the Red Belly* (all published by Wolfhound Press). She works in Trinity College Library, Dublin.

David Caddy was born in 1962. As a child he loved travelling around Western Australia with the ten members of his family. He also loved mashed potato, swimming and picking his toenails. As an adult, he still loves his family (now vastly extended), travel, mashed potato and swimming, and he really loves writing. (He still picks his toenails.)

David's first book, *Whammy*, was published in 1996, and his new novel, *Smash*, was published in 2000.

Jenny Coote always wanted to be a surfer and went to the beach near her home nearly every day. In her final year at school, she entered her story, 'BIG Weekend', in a creative writing competition, and was named runner-up to the winner. She is now studying to be an architect and has not written any more stories — but maybe she will now!

Warren Flynn. Due to low marks in physics, and a long weekend with two Bob Dylan albums, Warren Flynn decided not to become an engineer. He started writing poems and stories at high school and hasn't stopped since. He's also taught plenty of English, designed tee-shirts, studied Indonesian, and tutored guitar in a maximum security prison. He lives with his wife on the southern coast of Western Australia, near Albany.

Flynn's novels, *Gaz*, *Different Voices*, and *Gaz Takes Off* are relished by teenagers throughout Australia. These contemporary adventures, spiced with humour and pathos, encourage readers to embrace tolerance and hope. They are used as class texts in many schools. All three have been short-listed by teenagers for the West Australian Young Readers' Book Award. *Different Voices* was also short-listed for the West Australian Premier's Prize. Flynn's newest work, *Escaping Paradise*, set in Bali and Java, will surprise and challenge his fans.

Elaine Forrestal lives in Scarborough, Western Australia. Now that her two daughters live in far flung Melbourne and England she shares the dog and the cat with her husband, who is also a writer.

Elaine has had magazine articles and short stories published and has written for children's television. Her first novel, *The Watching Lake*, was shortlisted for the Western Australian Premier's Book Awards, and her second novel, *Someone Like Me* won the Children's Book Council Book of the Year Award (Younger Readers), the WAYBRA Hoffman Award and was Highly Commended in the NASEN Children's Book Awards in the UK. Two new novels, *Straggler's Reef* and *Graffiti on the Fence* have recently been released.

Cora Harrison taught primary-school children in England for twenty-five years before moving to a small farm in Kilfenora, County Clare. The farm includes an Iron Age fort, with the remains of a small castle inside it, and the mysterious atmosphere of this ancient place gave Cora the idea for a series of historical novels tracing the survival of the ringfort through the centuries, from the Iron Age to the present day. *The Viking at Drumshee*, Book 9 in her popular Drumshee Timeline Series (published by Wolfhound Press), will be published in spring 2000.

Deborah Lisson was born in Croydon, England and came to Australia (Sydney) as a migrant in 1962. She moved to Perth, Western Australia, with her husband Richard, in 1963. They later spent two years in Kalgoorlie before settling in Bunbury where they still live.

Deborah's first book, *The Devil's Own*, a novel for older children, was published in 1990. Since then she has written three other children's novels. Her latest, *Red Hugh*, a historical novel set in sixteenth century Ireland, was published in Australia and Ireland in 1999. Details of Deborah's other books may be found on her website: www.geo.net.au/~lissond.

John Newman and Jim Halligan. After their spaceship crashed on Earth (Newman was driving), John and Jim took the only course of action available to aliens stranded on this planet. They became teachers.

Having drunk the last of their rocket fuel, they turned to writing. Their first efforts were several much-loathed schoolbooks which turned our heroes into hate figures across the nation. *Fowl Play*, their first effort at children's fiction, made the two geniuses household names in lunatic asylums and chicken farms all over the planet. Encouraged by this huge success, Halligan and Newman bought a new pencil and wrote their second children's book, *Round the Bend*. *Fowl Deeds*, the eagerly awaited sequel to *Fowl Play*, will be published by Wolfhound Press in spring 2000.

Aislinn O'Loughlin. Award-winning teenage author Aislinn O'Loughlin is well known for her hilariously quirky and fast-paced reworkings of famous fairy tales. Her first book, *Cinderella's Fella*, was written when she was only fourteen; her second, *A Right Royal Pain: the True Story of Rumpelstiltskin* (selected as a White Raven book by international librarians), followed only a few months later. *The Emperor's Birthday Suit* and *Shak and the Beanstalk* were published in 1997, and *Fionn the Cool* in 1998 (all available from Wolfhound Press). Ainslinn lives in Templeogue and is studying at University College, Dublin.

Larry O'Loughlin is a storyteller and author of five books for younger children; he is also co-author of *Our House*, a non-fiction book for adults. One of his titles for younger children, *The Goban Saor*, illustrated by John Leonard, was short-listed for the 1997 Bisto Book of the Year Award. His first book for teenagers, *Is Anybody Listening?*, was published by Wolfhound Press in 1999. Larry lives in Dublin with his wife and family. He is the father of author Aislinn O'Loughlin.

Mark O'Sullivan is the acclaimed author of the best-selling *Melody for Nora* (winner of the Eilis Dillon Memorial Award, short-listed for the 1995 Reading Association of Ireland Award, and selected as a White Raven book by international librarians); *Wash-Basin Street Blues*, also a bestseller; *More Than a Match*; *White Lies*, also selected as a White Raven book; *Angels Without Wings*, winner of the 1999 Reading Association of Ireland Award; and *Silent Stones* (all published by Wolfhound Press). Four of his novels have been nominated for the Bisto Book of the Year Award, and his work has been translated into six languages. Mark lives in Thurles, County Tipperary, with his wife and two daughters.

Kim Scott is a descendant of people who have always lived along the south-east coast of Western Australia and is glad to be one among those who call themselves Nyoongar. Kim has published two novels, *True Country* and *Benang*, and his poetry and short stories have appeared in a range of anthologies. 'Dallas' Dad' is his first story for younger readers.